Just for the Birds

by

Jinx Schwartz

JUST FOR THE BIRDS
Published by Jinx Schwartz
Copyright 2018
Book 10: Hetta Coffey series
All rights reserved.

JUST FOR THE BIRDS

A Mexican walks into a bar, with a parrot on his shoulder.

The bartender asks, "Where did you get that thing?"

The parrot replies, "In Mexico. There are millions of them!"

Chapter One

YOU JUST KNOW it's gonna be a crappy afternoon when you return from grocery shopping to find your boat's deck crawling with armed men.

Okay, so they were at least uniformed armed men, but the Mexican police?

Break out the foulies, matey! Extreme dung storm dead ahead!

I'd noticed an unmanned *Policia* car parked in the marina lot, lights still flashing, but I figured they were just taking a beer break at The Dock Café. Then I saw where they really *were* and my solar plexus twitched. Mine is a little too well-padded to actually flex, but it spasmed. I burped cinnamon and cayenne pepper. Maybe I shouldn't have inhaled that triple-scoop dulce de leche ice cream earlier, what with my slight lactose intolerance.

And then there's this love/hate relationship I have with the local authorities; they would dearly love to throw me in the slammer, and I'd truly hate that.

Luckily, I have friends South of the border in both

authoritative *and* low places. It's a Mexico thing.

Halfway down the ramp, I heard my golden retriever, Po Thang, yelping, "Help!"

You know how it is with dogs, they have distinctive barks for different situations, and his frantic yelping did not bode well for whatever this one was. I'd left him inside my forty-five-foot motor vessel, *Raymond Johnson*, with the doggy door locked so he couldn't go walkabout while I went for victuals. Since it was an unusually warm January morning in southern Baja, I'd even left the air conditioning on low to make sure he was comfortable. The ungrateful little cur was nonetheless miffed at being left behind, but at least he was safe. Or so I'd thought.

Leaving my dock cart full of goodies where it was, I raced—okay, fast-walked, which I consider racing—for my boat.

Four cops were on my deck, tugging on the locked sliding hatch into my main cabin. Several curious cruisers stood around calmly watching the show, and since I didn't smell or see smoke, at least the fear that my pooch was trapped on my burning boat dissipated somewhat. I took a deep breath and strode toward the boat just as one of the cops spotted me. "*¡Señora! You* dog! What is wrong with she?"

I'd long ago given up correcting Mexicans who, because of my advanced age, just assumed I must be married. And this was certainly no time to get into pronoun usage. "*No se, Señor.* I wish I *did* know." I turned to face the growing crowd of boaters. "Anyone see anything?"

They all shook their heads, but one cruiser said, "Not me. Your dog just went nuts inside your boat, and we couldn't get in to find out why."

"Stand by!" I yelled as I stomped up my resin boarding steps onto the boat. Everyone took a step back, including the police officers, who looked vastly relieved I was taking charge. Clearly, dealing with a snarling, howling, and obviously deranged dog wasn't in their pay grade.

Unlocking the slider, I moved it open six inches. "Po Thang! Are you all right, Sweetie?"

Sixty-five pounds of Sweetie slammed into the teak slider and I was barely able to hold the door to that small opening. Hoping I didn't lose a finger in the process, I grabbed his collar to hold him in place. His howls of fury turned into whines, so I held fast while I pushed the door wide to pull him outside.

At least, that was *my* plan. Po Thang obviously had other ideas. He yanked backward, jerking me into the cabin and almost dislocating my shoulder. As I disappeared through the door, my peripheral vision spotted all four cops brandishing their guns.

What were they gonna do? Shoot *me* in the ass? Lord knows even the worst marksman could hardly miss a target that big.

Po Thang, reduced to small yips now that I was close, was still breathing hard and struggling against my tenuous grip on his collar. My slick hand had gone numb and pain ran up my arm in electric shock waves. Soaking with sweat from the struggle, I was losing patience, fast.

"Sit!" I bellowed, punctuating the command with a sharp downward index finger stab that stopped just short of his nose.

Shocked by this unusually harsh and loud demand, he froze and plopped his furry butt down on the carpet. Which left us both bewildered. I had to remember that one.

Grabbing his leash from a hook by the door, I clipped it onto his collar and secured the other end to my stainless-steel wheel on the lower steering station.

Kneeling in front of the still-sitting, whining dog, I ran my hands over his body. Not finding any obvious injuries, I took his head in my hands, planning to give him a serious talking to, but blood on his nose made me gasp. "Oh, my precious pup. What on earth have you done to yourself?"

He dawg-sniveled and tried to paw his nose, but I held him tightly. Looking around, I saw a hand towel I normally use to clean off my feet before entering the cabin and managed, despite my dry mouth, to spit on it. Wiping carefully, I saw he had a small wound on the end of his nose, and another on his ear.

"You been in a prizefight, Furface?"

He cocked his head and gave me a silly Golden Retriever grin.

I interpreted this to mean, "You shoulda seen the other guy."

Chapter Two

AFTER CHECKING PO THANG over again for wounds, I was satisfied that the ear tear and nose scratch were it. But what had happened to him?

The main cabin—or saloon, or salon, both pronounced like a beauty salon—had been redecorated with an egg beater. Couch cushions were strewn hither and thither, chairs knocked over, Po Thang's water dish upside down, and for some unexplainable reason a bag of dog food, which Po Thang had never touched (why should he when he had a perfectly stocked refrigerator?) was torn open and kibble was everywhere.

The evidence pointed to my spoiled rotten dog pitching a hissy fit and raging separation anxiety when I left him alone, or he had gotten himself tangled up in something and had a hell of a struggle getting free. "You'd better pray to whatever dog god you can that it was the latter, or you are destined to be caged whenever I leave this boat in the future."

He looked guilty and pleaded the fifth.

Dragging him outside, I asked if anyone had a first-aid kit handy. I didn't want to leave Po Thang alone long enough to go back inside for mine, and besides, now that the hound from hell had been removed, the cops asked my permission to check the boat's interior for possible intruders.

Herding Po Thang onto the dock, I grabbed a hose and, of course, he balked. What is it with a Golden Retriever who'll happily take an illegal dive into the swimming pool at a first-class resort at the drop of a hat, and then freaks out at the prospect of being squirted with a hose? Once he realized I was just washing my hands and wetting a towel, he politely sat while I wiped away the quickly drying blood from his nose and ear.

Cruisers gathered around, petting and baby-talking him while speculating how he'd been injured. Getting all that attention being right up Po Thang's alley, he played the pity card to the hilt, spurring his adoring public to fetch tasty tidbits to soothe his distress. In between chomping on goodies, he cut dirty looks back at the boat and grumped.

"¡Madre de Dios!"

"¡Chingado!"

The cops' shouts preceded a hasty and clumsy retreat, all of them trying to get through the narrow door at the same time. As the last officer backed out, he came close to tripping and landing on his butt while swatting wildly at something with his hat. Slamming the door shut, he took a moment to put on his cap and pull down his jacket in an attempt to regain a modicum of dignity before turning to face the crowd of amused looky-loos.

Once safely back on the dock, the policemen held a whispered conference, drew their guns and looked as though preparing to shoot up my boat. Since a boat full of holes is a really bad thing, I released the brake on Po Thang's leash and jumped back on deck.

Po Thang followed. "Wooooooaaaahhh! Wooooooooooooo!"

"Hush." I tapped him lightly on the snout, and he lowered his howl level a mite. Just enough so I heard a familiar sound from inside.

"Oh, ya got trouble, folks, right here in River City," screeched the perpetrator.

I threw my arms out, hands in a traffic cop signal. "No!Stop! *¡Alto!*" I yelled at the cops.

They had no problem *alto*-ing; going back inside that hell ship was the last thing they wanted to do. They held their ground and for the first time I noticed a bright green feather on one cop's hat, and another floating above our heads.

I handed Po Thang's leash to a cruiser and boarded *Raymond Johnson*, prepared to give the known mischief-maker a good talking to, but when I stepped inside he was cowering and shivering behind a pillow on the settee, mumbling to himself.

Picking him up, I cuddled him to my chest and cooed, "Oh, Trouble. You poor thing. What on earth has happened to you, baby bird?"

He shook and cluck/chuffed weakly in distress. My heart melted.

Wrapping him in a chenille throw from the couch, I

hugged him tighter in case he had any ideas of taking flight, slid the door open and stuck my head outside. "Everything's okay. It's just a parrot. *My* parrot. He flew in through porthole like he used to do, I guess."

One of La Paz's finest mumbled something like, "Devil bird," and they stomped away as fast as they could. The guy holding Po Thang's leash asked, above furious barks, "Uh, what should I do with this fella?"

"Can you take him for a walk, please? I have to make some phone calls."

"Well, I was…."

Another cruiser, a woman who owned a poodle friend of Po Thang's, stepped forward. "I've got him, Hetta. Call me on the radio when you're ready for him to come home, okay?"

"I owe you big time, Karen. Okay folks, show's over. Thank all of you for your help and concern."

Back inside, I gave Trouble water and a portion of my coveted Oh Boy! Oberto! turkey jerky, his favorite. Instead of attacking the jerky like a shark on chum in his usual modus operandi, he feebly nibbled on it and let it fall. I was tempted to grab it for myself, but instead I added a jalapeño pepper and an apple slice to his dish. He pecked at both without any real interest. Alarmed at both the way he looked and was acting, I called my BFF, Jan.

"Hey, Hetta. What's up?"

"Our Trouble is back."

"Our? Our? Hetta, Hetta, Hetta. I am perpetually amazed at your capacity for two things: downing adult beverages, and somehow sharing, or should I say, *ensnaring*, me into whatever mess you have gotten yourself into. Trouble? Gee, what a shock. It's. What. You. Do. And why is it *our* trouble?"

One of the things I've loved most about Jan for over twenty years is her willingness to sign up for new adventures. Okay, so most times I do drag her into my debacles kicking and screaming, but eventually she dives in with great enthusiasm.

"What are the chances of you coming down here? I'm kinda in a jam."

"Again, nothing new there. But, yes! A thousand times over, yes! Any excuse, even one of your fiascos, to get the hell out of this piece of crap fish camp. I hardly see Chino anymore, anyhow. Whales are arriving in droves this year."

"I think that's pods. Jan, Chino's a scientist. A world renowned marine biologist. It's his *job* to count whales. What do you expect from him?"

"If you're gonna go all preacherly on me, I sure as hell ain't gonna make an eight-hour drive to La Paz."

"Sorry, I'm just a little frustrated right now. Please, pretty please with sugar on it, can you get down here, like, ASAP?" I begged. Then as an added incentive I told her, "I just bought a case of Malbec."

"Why didn't you just say so in the first place? I can't make it before dark tonight, but if I leave soon I can get as far as Mulege before I gotta get a room."

"Good thinking, just promise me you'll stick to the rules, Chica." All gringos know better than to drive at night on Mexico's Highway One, but Jan and I have been known to push that boundary in a pinch. "I'm good until you get here. I've farmed Po Thang out for the night. Oh, and please throw a cage into your Jeep, okay?"

"Sure. Wait. Why did you ban the dawg, why a cage, and how big?"

"Ha! I knew you couldn't get off the phone without details." I brought her up to speed on the return of Trouble and the ensuing dustup.

"Oh, no. Poor Trouble."

"Actually, I think he got the best of el dawg. Po Thang's sporting a couple of minor wounds. Trouble's sleeping now, but he looks like he's gone a round or two with something meaner than him before he even met Po Thang. I gotta call Craig, and I'll send you a text with photos of Trouble for Dr. Chino to take a look at. We can't have too many veterinarians on the case."

"I'll make sure he sees the pics before I leave for La Paz. He's got a soft spot for Trouble, as you know, even if they did get off to a somewhat rocky start. If it wasn't high whale migration season, I know he'd come down with me. I gotta get busy and hit the road so I can get there early tomorrow. *Hasta mañana.*"

"Call me when you've stopped for the night, okay? I don't want to have to worry about you *and* Trouble."

She laughed. "Gee, your concern for me is overwhelming."

"You know what I mean. Drive careful now, y'all," I drawled, mimicking our Texas parents. "Keep it between the bar ditches."

After I hung up I said aloud, "Not that there are any bar ditches in Baja. The roads don't even have shoulders."

Trouble, who looked as though he'd been in a debilitated state long before his run-in with Po Thang and the cops, finally gave up picking at his food, tucked his head under a tattered wing, and fell asleep again with a tiny piece of jerky still in his beak.

I wrapped him in on old tee shirt, and got my phone again so I could send the pictures out to everyone concerned. He barely peeped as I uncovered him for closeups. The more I looked him over, the more my concern increased. He felt light as a feather, was missing some, and was semi-covered in some kind of oily substance. After I rewrapped him and put him on the couch, I texted the photos to Doctor Brigido Camacho Yee, a.k.a. Chino—who is not only a marine biologist, but a vet to boot—at the whale camp, then called Doctor Craig Washington, DVM, in Arizona.

"Hey, Hetta. What's new?"

"Trouble's back."

"I asked if there was anything *new*."

Was I detecting a pattern here?

However this wasn't the time to defend my reputation. That was a lost cause anyhow. "No, Trouble, my monk parrot. I put him into a bird sanctuary here in the Baja for his own good, and he seemed okay there. Okay, so he was a bully, lording it over what he considered his lesser species inside the aviary, but he eventually settled down. Sort of. Anyhow, he's suddenly appeared back at my boat and he looks like holy hell."

"I'm sorry to hear that. Is he obviously injured?"

"Not that I can see. I texted you photos a minute ago."

"I'll check them out and call you right back. Is he eating or drinking anything?"

"A little. He drank some water, then ate part of a jalapeño pepper, a couple of bites of jerky, and a nibble of apple. He's snoring to beat the band right now."

"Hmmm. Not like him at all to leave food."

"I'm not sure, but he may have ripped open a bag and eaten some of Po Thang's dry dog food before I fed him. Is that going to be a problem?"

"Shouldn't be. I'll be back with you in a flash."

I hung up and listened to Trouble's bird snores. They seemed normal, if a little on the weak side. When the phone barked, I snatched it up and Craig asked, "Is there a bird vet down there?"

His question frightened me. "Not that I know of, but I can check around."

"Let me do that from here. What's he doing right now?"

"Still sleeping."

"In his cage?"

"No, Jan's bringing one."

"Are his wings clipped?"

"Nope."

"Okay, get one of Jenk's socks, cut out the toe, and slip it over him for right now. We have to keep him immobile and warm."

"Me and what army?"

"He trusts you. Give it a shot."

"You gonna cover my doctor bills?"

He laughed. "Sounds like he's not up to his usual mayhem."

"You want to bet? You should see my main cabin."

"How's Po Thang taking to him?"

"Not. Evidently, World War Three broke out aboard *Raymond Johnson*. Po Thang has a bloody nose, an ear bite, and a great loss of dignity. He's on another boat for now, and Jan'll be here tomorrow."

"Maybe I spoke too soon about mayhem. Do your best to keep him quiet and toasty. I'll do some more research and get back to you tomorrow morning. Meanwhile, don't worry too much, I think once Trouble is rested up and eating normally, he'll be fine."

He hung up.

I raided that case of wine.

Chapter Three

JAN ARRIVED IN time for lunch.

I was already frazzled.

My morning started early, with Trouble screeching while struggling with his sock-swaddling restraint I'd sneaked over him while he was dozing in my lap the night before. I'd put him in a towel-lined cardboard box next to my bed, but was awakened by curses and squawks as he did a fair job of ripping up Jenks's sock that I'd already cut up, and the box.

I finished un-swaddling him, and once he was free he gave me a nip to let me know he was not pleased. He immediately took to the air, squawking to beat the band. I tried bribing him with jerky to hush his bird-cusses, but his shrieks must have echoed throughout my end of the marina, as I heard the unmistakable barks of my dog carrying on a light breeze.

Quickly leaving the boat, I rushed to spring Po Thang for a walk and breakfast at the Dock Café. He was somewhat pacified by scrambled eggs and bacon, but kept shooting me dirty looks. He ate most of my breakfast for

I was distracted, ears cocked for screeching, which seemed to have ceased for the time being.

When my dog finished off my toast, I walked him back to his keepers. As we passed *Raymond Johnson*, he let out a low growl. "Suck it up, Buttercup," I growled back.

Handing his leash over to Karen, I apologized profusely for the early wakeup, but she waved me off. "Not to worry, he was a good boy for the most part. Until your parrot let loose this morning."

"I'm sorry about that. Guess I won't be voted Best Dock Mate of the Week. The truth is, though, I'm a little relieved that Trouble's even feeling well enough to raise a ruckus."

"He's sick?"

"Not sure. He looks awful and just picks at his food. Even jerky! He's just not himself. I've called a couple of veterinarian friends of mine to look into it. Hopefully I'll be able to fetch Po Thang later today, since Jan's on her way."

"That should send the entire male population of the marina into a frenzy of deck projects, just in case she walks by. Nothing like a tall, blue-eyed blonde to make their day."

"True, that. Anyhow, between Jan and me, we'll come with up a plan. If all else fails, I'll send either Trouble or Po Thang home with her. Meanwhile, I may have to call on your hubby to build a peace wall down the center of my boat."

"Ha! I'd rather keep Po Thang indefinitely rather than send Kevin down to your boat with Jan on board," she teased.

Back on *Raymond Johnson*, I found Trouble dozing, but noticed he'd finished his jerky. I collapsed on the settee, planning on a short nap, but remembrances of how Trouble entered my life the first time kept me awake.

I was taking a siesta aboard *Raymond Johnson* at Marina Real, in San Carlos, Sonora, that day, not all that long after I arrived in Mexico. Jenks had returned to the Middle East, leaving me to work on a project—a feasibility assessment on Sea of Cortez ports—for my on-again-off-again employer, Wontrobski, A.K.A. The Trob.

I am Hetta Coffey, CEO, CFO, president, and sole employee of Hetta Coffey, SI, LLC. The SI is my little inside joke on the phonetic pronunciation of Civil Engineer.

A single woman of forty—yes, I can actually say that now without requiring heart defibrillation—I'm an engineer by degree who stays somewhat employed thanks to a penchant for engaging in, shall we say, much less than run-of-the-mill endeavors.

My best friend of many years, Jan, says I tread heavily upon the felonious side of life, but what does she know? She's a CPA who's flipping tortillas for her honey at a whale camp. At least I get paid.

Perpetually single, I actually have a wonderful—but too often absent—man in my life. Jenks Jenkins works in Dubai and I live in Mexico. When we are together, all is well, but left on my own, I teeter on the brink of blowing the best relationship I've ever had because I'm bullheaded and as temperamental as any Texas redhead. I prefer to think of myself as self-governing, but according to Jan I'm doing that even worse than the U.S. Congress. She says I'm stubborn, incorrigible, and morally corrupt, which is why she likes me so much.

One can clearly see why Jan and I are like sisters.

I live aboard my 45-foot motor yacht, Raymond Johnson, named for my dearly departed dog, RJ. Living aboard in the lap of luxury compared to many of my fellow cruisers, my boat is outfitted with wall to wall marine blue carpeting throughout, a large master cabin with a queen-sized bed, spacious head with shower, another cabin for guests (with their own head), state-of-the-art galley with a dinette I use for my office, and every bell and whistle a yacht of this size should have. I can anchor out for long periods and still have all the comforts of landlubbers and dock dwellers; they are just a little harder to maintain. My eight KW generator, multiple solar panels, inverter, large battery bank, and several five-gallon propane tanks, give me the ability to make fresh water from sea water, air condition and heat my cabins, cook, and make ice. These luxuries come at the price of constant maintenance and gallons of diesel but are worth the time and expense.

The only drawback is that Jenks, the wonderful man I'm in love with, works in the Middle East and though we do see each other often, it can get a little lonely at times.

Anyhow, at present, Po Thang and I were parked at the dock in La Paz, Mexico, but that was not the usual case. I'd spent most of my time cruising around in the Central

Sea of Cortez, where I managed to stay employed. Not always exactly safely or legally employed, mind you, but I'd made enough to keep us in kibble and refrieds.

Back when I worked as a project engineer for large corporations, I traveled the world, stayed in five-star hotels, and ate and drank high on the hog, thanks to a fat expense account. Those days are but a memory, thank goodness. I much prefer living aboard my boat in Mexico's spectacular Sea, drinking cocolocos and eating tacos. The downside is missing Jenks and scrambling for work to keep my head above water.

Literally.

But I digress.

Back to **The Day of Trouble**, as I now refer to it. It is much more amusing in hindsight, but at the time, I was *not* amused.

I'd settled in for my habitual afternoon siesta, and just drifted off, when someone rapped on my hull. A hanging offense in my book.

"¡Day Hache Elle!"

I tried to ignore it, thinking it was a vendor selling shrimp, lobster, or whatever. They'd be back at a more reasonable hour, I was certain.

The pounding increased and I stomped to my teak slider.

Willing myself into what passed for consciousness, I staggered out onto the deck, primed to strangle anyone with the nerve to disturb my sacred siesta period. Two beaming men in red and yellow shirts stood on the dock. One held a matching yellow clipboard.

"*Buenas tardes, Señora. Day Hache Elle.*"

"What do you want? *Uh, que quieres?*" My Spanish sucks, but I can make myself understood.

"*¿Usted es Señora Café?*"

"*No, soy* Señorita Hetta Coffey." Back then I was still trying to convince the locals that I was a Miss instead of a Mrs., but it was an uphill slog. Evidently Mexican women are married well before pushing thirty-nine. Now that I've fallen over the forty cliff, I've given up.

He thrust the clipboard at me and indicated I sign by the X. It was then I saw who they were, DHL. Figuring that Wontrobski, the man who keeps me in projects and thereby rice and beans, had messengered paperwork, I signed and held out my hand for a package, but received the Mexican thumb and forefinger hand signal that means anything from, wait a minute to I'll be right back. It was the latter, for they both left.

Thirsty, I went inside for a glass of water and when I returned, the men were lugging a large box down the dock. Actually, not a box, a crate. Actually, not a crate, a cage. From it emanated an unearthly screech, followed by earsplitting, but recognizable, lyrics. "Ack! Oh, ya got trouble, folks/right here in River City..."

Trouble had arrived. Starts with a T, ends with an E.

Flummoxed, I bribed the DHL guys with a beer, and slugged one down myself, all the while trying to figure out how to get rid of the pesky parrot. Several Tecates later, between my Spanish and their almost non-existent English, I finally obtained a phone number in Hermosillo. Since getting a Mexican cellphone was on my list for the next day, I was forced to fire up my million peso a minute satellite phone.

"*Day Hache Elle*," a woman answered.

"Do you speak English?"

"*Sí.*"

"Okay, here's the deal. I've received a shipment I don't want. I want to send it back."

"Back?"

"*Sí. Uh, devolver.* Return to sender." Elvis sang in my head, but I suspected I *knew* the address, for certain.

"*Momentito, por favor.*"

Very expensive *momentitos* ensued. I ticked off the ka-chings while watching the delivery guys raid my refrigerator for more Tecate. I signaled for them to bring me one. It was half gone when there was a click. I thought maybe the connection was cut, and almost hung up when a hearty, unaccented, voice boomed, "DHL. Can I help you?"

"Oh, thank God. Yes, you can. I just received a shipment I don't want. How do I send it back where it came from?"

"Bill of Lading number?"

I grabbed my copy and read off the numbers. It was then I noticed the critter was definitely, as I had suspected, from my mother in Texas, and recalled a conversation about some bird my aunt had taken in.

"Can you hold?" he asked but didn't wait for my answer. Ka-ching! More expensive satellite phone time, with the added insult of scratchy elevator music. The parrot sang along.

One of my yellow-shirted new best friends popped another top and handed me a bottle.

What seemed an eternity later, I heard, "Miss Coffey?"

"That would be me."

"You are in Mexico?"

"Yes I am."

"Why is it that you don't want the box of jerky?"

"Jerky? I didn't get jerky, I received a parrot."

"A parrot? I don't understand. We have suspended bird shipments in both directions temporarily, what with the bird flu thing."

"Look, Buster, I don't know what the hell you're trying to pull off here. These two guys showed up with a damned parrot and I don't want the little bugger."

"Miss Coffey, there's no need to get upset. What does your manifest say you received?"

I squinted at the blurry writing, rummaged for a pair of reading glasses and finally made it out. "*Caso de la machaca.*"

"What's that?"

"Hell, I don't know. Hold on, I'll get my Spanish to English dictionary."

I did. Machaca: dried meat. Dammit. "Okay, I found it. A machaca is a rare Mexican parrot."

"Miss Coffey, I don't think so. However, you only have to refuse the shipment."

Now, why didn't I think of that? "So if I do, will these guys take the, uh, machaca back to Hermosillo? I mean, they won't just put it in a warehouse somewhere, will they?" I conjured a vision of this cute, if noisy, bird dying a slow horrible death by starvation. Hunger is something I avoid at all costs.

"How would I know? I'm in New Jersey."

No amount of beer would convince the guys to reload Trouble into their truck.

After all, they pointed out, I had signed for the shipment and they must leave, now that I was getting low on Tecate.

My normally not-at-all treacherous mother had figured out a way to ship the pesky parrot she'd gotten stuck with. from Texas to Mexico. It was my least favorite Aunt Lillian who fobbed the bird off on Mom and Dad, and now he was my problem.

And, I was out of beer.

And now Trouble had landed once again in my life.

I checked the time; Jenks, an early riser, would be up and at 'em in Dubai by now. My long-distance sig-other picked up on the first ring. "Hey, Red. I was just getting ready to call you. I miss you."

"Great minds and all. I miss you, too."

"Seems like forever since I was there on the boat, but it's only been a couple of weeks."

"Twelve days, three hours."

"Not that anyone's counting, right?"

We shared a laugh, then I said, "Uh, I have a problem."

"Already? You need bail money?"

"Very funny. I am in need of a birdcage. Uh, and by

the way, you are short one sock."

"Let me guess. Another of my favorite Navy socks has once again disappeared?"

I grinned. Those polyester Navy issue socks were indeed mysteriously meeting with accidents in the laundry. "You mean those baby-doo-doo colored, mustard-brown-yellow polyester horrors you are so fond of? Nope, I think they've all gone walk about. Besides, I needed something cotton and fashionable. Trouble has standards, you know."

"I'm intrigued. I feel a story coming on."

"Yes. Trouble has arrived."

"So, what else is new?"

Yep, there was for sure a pattern here.

"Trouble, my Quaker parrot. He's back. He flew in this morning."

"You pick him up at the airport?"

That made me laugh out loud, something I badly needed to do. I sighed again, told him thanks for being there for me, and all about my crappy day. And why the demise of his sock.

"Went for a good cause. Poor Trouble. You think he's sick?"

"More like rode hard and put away wet."

"Did you call the bird sanctuary where you left him for safe keeping? Obviously, they aren't doing a great job of it."

"Called twice. No answer. I left a message for Humberto, the caretaker, to call me back. Jan's on her way to help with the bird versus hound problem, thank goodness. And I've sent photos of Trouble to both Craig and Chino, two of the best veterinarians in the entire world, in my humble opinion. I'm just so worried about the poor little thing."

"Hetta, he's safe now as long as Po Thang is farmed out. Trouble'll be fine. He's one tough hombre, as you well know."

I did know that. Because of his singing and talking abilities, we figured Trouble was once a pet, but by the time my aunt found him, he was a wild street scrapper. But then, most Monk parrots are. It's their constant loud squabbling that makes them unpopular as neighbors. That, and causing power outages by several mating pairs building large, elaborate nests that cause damage to electrical lines and utility poles. Those nests allow them to survive the cold winters in the northern United States, much to the dismay of many a neighborhood. And removing their sturdily crafted homes is an exercise in futility; they are known to rebuild within an hour.

My Aunt Lillian, who I consider a giant pain in the keister, had saved him from a gang fight. Several large Texas blue jays, well known for their own cantankerousness, were set on giving him a shellacking, but he was holding his own when she got tired of all the noise and shooed them off. She offered Trouble a treat and he adopted her. That alone shows he's a lousy judge of character.

Anyhow, after she heard him sing his signature song, she named him Trouble, then dumped him on my dad when she took off with hubby number whatever on a honeymoon. So, then my parents dumped him on me, and I dumped him on the bird sanctuary. Poor bird probably has an identity problem.

After Jenks and I said our goodbyes, I hung up and eyed my scraggly-looking dumpee. "I feel your pain, as I too, am feeling unwanted. And we're both unemployed. At least you've lost weight."

"Ack! Trouble is a pretty bird."

Chapter Four

AFTER MY CHAT with Jenks, I cuddled up with Trouble on the couch and finally zonked out.

"Hetta! Wake up! The cavalry has arrived!"

I startled awake, as did Trouble, who broke into his rendition of "The Yellow Rose of Texas" when he heard Jan's voice.

She left a cage on deck, rushed inside, gently picked up Trouble and held him close. "Oh, you poor baby. What on earth has happened to my handsome boy? Hetta, what is this…slime…all over him?"

"I don't know."

"Can he fly?"

"Sure can. Judging by my dog's nose and ear injuries, he was up for one hell of an aerial dog fight."

Jan laughed. "I'd liked to have seen that. Probably something akin to King Kong versus the bi-plane scene."

Trouble scurried up onto Jan's shoulder, leaned against her neck, and dozed off again.

I hugged her, careful not to dislodge Trouble. If you think I can be a stone bitch when someone wakes me, I can't hold a candle to that bird.

"Jan, I can't thank you enough for coming down. What did Chino have to say about the photos I sent of Trouble?"

"He's puzzled. For sure, this little bird has been in some kind of, you should excuse the expression, trouble. He and Craig were going to have a telephone confab this morning."

My phone barked, and I picked it up. "Speak of the devil. Hey, Craig. Jan just got here. What did you and Chino come up with?"

I put him on speaker so Jan could hear. "Not much. Is the patient better today?"

"Still looks like hell, and weary, but he is eating a little and drinking lots of water. He was always a feather weight, but I swear he's lost a few ounces."

"Ha! Chino said Trouble looks a mite green around the gills."

Jan and I giggled. Leave it to a British-educated Mexican marine biologist to say that about a parrot.

"Have you, by any chance found a bird veterinarian in La Paz?" Craig asked.

"I asked on the cruiser's news this morning but didn't have any luck. Does Chino know of one?"

"He's on the case. Why does Trouble appear sweaty, or wet, in the photos?"

Jan piped up. "He's not wet. He's greasy. Can we give him a bath? He loves them."

"He's oily? Or do you think it's some kind of grease?" Craig asked.

"Kinda looks like vegetable oil."

"Okay, try this first. Just make him a shallow warm-water bath and let him do his thing. Then shower him off. If that doesn't remove the grease, then we'll try a couple of drops of Dawn in the water when I get there. I'll be in La Paz tomorrow, so try the plain water thing, but make certain the boat is warm, and draft free. Don't dry him off...I want him to preen."

"You're coming to La Paz?"

"As soon as I can get there, which is tomorrow."

Jan and I cheered. Trouble opened one eye, grumbled, and went right back to sleep.

"I'll pick you up at the airport," I said. "What time does your plane arrive?"

"I'm flying into San Diego, then catching Volaris from Tijuana to La Paz. My connection is a little tight, but if I make it, I'll be there around eight-thirty your time. What hotel would you recommend?"

"You don't need one. I have the keys to my friend Rhonda's condo that is right next to the marina. She's gone for a month. And there's a bonus; you get Po Thang, as well."

"Oh, grand."

He sounded like he meant it.

Silly boy.

We ran about two inches of warm water in the kitchen sink and Trouble jumped right in. He splashed, shook, dunked his head, flapped his wings, and stopped occasionally to preen. Soaking wet, he looked downright pitiful. I tested the water temp, turned on the spray in the other basin, then showered him while draining the sink.

All that activity taxed what little strength he had, so with one last half-hearted shake, he promptly fell asleep. I wrapped him in a towel and called Craig to ask him if I could use my hairdryer on low to finish the job.

"Absolutely not. That's a draft, in my book, warm or not. Just wrap him in a series of warm dry towels until he dries out. Pat, don't rub. Is he still greasy?"

"Hard to tell. The feathers on his head, the ones he has left, seem to be fluffing up."

"Good. See you tomorrow and try not to worry too much, okay?"

"Uh, Craig, the fact that you're flying down here to examine him? That means I probably have plenty to worry about."

"Nah, just using Trouble as an excuse to head for Mexico. It was twenty-six degrees here this morning. Oh, and Roger is coming, as well."

I glanced at a photo of Craig and Roger on my desk. Both were dressed in western duds, and not the drugstore kind. Craig, tall-black-and-handsome, and Roger, a little shorter, white, and weathered from years of ranching, mugged for the camera, their arms draped over each other's shoulders. They made a Marlboro Man meets *La Cage aux Folle* kind of couple.

"Even better. We'll have your condo, and dog, ready for you. *Hasta luego, hombre.*"

I tried reaching the bird sanctuary again, but no luck. I

went online to see if I could learn anything, and found an article on the Pronatura website that the entire ranch had been purchased by some conservancy group out of Mexico City. I was looking for a contact number for that agency when Jan, who was on the hunt on her own laptop across the table from me, said, "Hey, Chica. You gotta see this. Sending now."

I waited impatiently for her find to travel the two entire feet from her Dell to my HP. It only took three minutes, but in this day and age we expect instantaneous results. Like, I didn't eat breakfast, so does that mean I've lost weight today? In my dreams.

After reading the purloined missive, I was shocked to learn Trouble might be worth way more than his weight in gold.

"Good grief, Janster. Smuggling parrots is more profitable than marijuana these days. The markup on Mexican marijuana is about a hundred percent. A pound of pot in Mexico costs around seventy bucks and resells in the States for double that. The profit margin on a double yellow head *starts* at three hundred percent. Who knew?"

Jan caught me sizing up my bedraggled bird. "Forget it. Trouble ain't no double yellow head. In fact, I'm not sure you could even sell his breed up north, so get those dollar signs out of your greedy little head."

Jeez, that woman knows me all too well. "*Au contraire*, Miz smarty britches." I opened a bookmarked page on my PC and read, " 'Sweet baby monks, hand fed. Five hundred dollars.' "

"Trouble is far from sweet, and no baby."

"Yeah, but he talks and sings. He even made TV commercials for Oh, Boy! Oberto jerky for a while until a peck of PETA persons filed suit. Said jerky isn't good for parrots."

"And poor Trouble lost his job. Shades of that '*Yo quiero* Taco Bell' Chihuahua."

"I loved those commercials. Some PCer always spoils the fun for everyone," I lamented.

"Speaking of fun, isn't it official? Jenks isn't here to declare it, so I will."

"Official enough for me. Break out the booze, Chica."

"What a beautiful evening," Jan said as we sipped our tall drinks on the back deck.

We'd perfected our own concoctions based on cocolocos, made with fresh coconut water, a splash of coconut cream, sugar water, lime, and dark spiced rum. We added nutmeg and ginger juice. "I wonder what the poor folks are doing tonight?"

"Freezing their tails off. It even snowed in the Texas Hill Country yesterday."

"Always a treat when that happened when we were kids. Quarter of an inch, and they closed the schools. Phone."

According to my caller ID, the call was from Rancho Los Pajaros! I quickly answered and hit the speaker button so Jan could hear. "*¡Hola! Hum—*"

A gruff voice cut me short and rattled off something

in rapid Spanish.

"*Mande? Quien habla?*" I asked. I wanted to know what he said, and who was talking.

Silence. I thought they'd hung up, then I heard whispering in the background, and scuffling noises. A familiar voice asked, "*Señora Café?*"

"Yes! Humberto, is that you? Are you okay?"

The bird sanctuary caretaker said, "*Lo siento, Señora. No hablo ingles.*"

What the hell? Humberto speaks English very well. And, he is one of the few Mexican men who calls me *Señorita* instead of *Señora.*

"I am calling to tell…" I stopped. Something was rotten in Mexico. I turned up the volume and hit the recorder I keep next to the phone. "Uh, how is my little parrot, Trouble?" I asked in English.

In Spanish, he answered that Trouble was fine and happy, and playing well with his bird friends.

Jan gave me a cut-it-short sign by dragging her finger across her neck, so I started to say goodbye, but then said, "That's good. Please give my regards to your wife, Paula."

He said he would and hung up.

"What do you make of that?" I asked Jan, who was frowning. How the heck does she look good doing that?

"I smell a giant *zorrillo*."

"Ya think? Humberto *does* speak English, his wife's name isn't Paula, he always calls me *señorita* and Trouble sure as hell ain't there. Yep, skunk stink all over it."

"On top of that," Jan added, "even when he is there,

Trouble, taking after you, steadfastly refuses to make nice with those of his species."

I shot her the finger, but she continued. "In fact, he doesn't even acknowledge he *is* a bird. He much prefers human company and spends most of his time in the house with Humberto and Anna. Ya think we oughta call the cops?"

Realizing the ridiculousness of what she just said, the two of us broke into raucous laughter. Even Trouble weakly chuckled. No one in her right mind called the Mexican police for, well, any reason.

After we ran out of breath, Jan swiped tears from her cheeks. "Seriously, who we gonna call? Bird Busters?"

"We'll think of something. I'm worried about Humberto and Anna. I've heard of cartel thugs taking over entire villages, so who knows what's going on out there at the ranch?"

"We could drive up there and snoop," Jan suggested. "Uh, you *do* still have your gun, right?"

"Yep. Not only that, like I told you before, I'm legal now. Nacho arranged somehow for me to get a Mexican carry permit."

"Ya know, I've been thinking about that. What did he say when he gave it to you? Like, you work for him now, or something?"

"He said, and I'm quoting him now," I tried to replicate his low, velvety Spanish accent, " 'Café,' "—he calls me Café because he hasn't mastered Hetta—" 'this is not a license to kill.' "

"What did you say?"

"Rats."

"Did you ask him just how he arranged this almost impossible feat?"

"Ha! Like he'd *tell* me?"

"Righto. Why would anyone ask how Nacho does *anything*. But, maybe we should put a little buzz in his ear about Trouble, Humberto and Anna."

"Yeah, right. I'm sure he'd rush right into the fray. Nacho and Trouble hate each other. I don't want to involve him until we're certain we can't handle the problem ourselves. You *know* how he is."

"Yes," she said, all dreamy-like. "Handsome, in a criminal kind of way. Mysterious, with friends in low places. And, he has the hots for you."

I scoffed. "Must be why he keeps either trying to kill me, or save me from others so he can have the pleasure later? If you remember, after the little French debacle, he said not to ever call him again unless I stumbled into, or caused, a threat of an imminent nuclear attack on Mexico."

The phone barked, and Jan grabbed it. Craig and Roger had made their connection in Tijuana and would arrive in a couple of hours. She hung up and it barked again. This time she handed it to me. I hit the speaker, on the off chance it was Humberto.

"*Hola.*"

"Uh, *hola* back. Hetta, how nice to hear your voice."

Jan frowned and mimed, "Who?"

I rolled my eyes and grabbed my neck in a choking motion. "Well, hi there, Doctor Washington. How are you and Doctor Washington doing these days?" I sing-songed.

"Very well. Thank you dear, for asking. Actually, I wanted to let you know we're coming down to La Paz to see Doctor Washington while he's there. It's a surprise so don't tell him, please?"

Jan's mouth fell open, then she slapped her hand over it and rushed onto the deck to stifle a big har har. I was left to stumble through the conversation, suggesting La Perla when Doc Wash asked for the name of a good hotel. I ended the call as fast as I could. Jan was still hiccupping laughs when I joined her on deck.

"I'm glad you find this situation amusing, Miz Jan. What the hell are we going to do?"

"Have the Doctors Washington, of Atherton, ever *met* Roger? Do they know he even *exists*?"

"Far as I know, they are fully aware that their son, Doctor Washington, Junior, has a business partner in his large animal veterinary hospital and cattle ranch."

"More like a *monkey*-bidness podner."

Jan stayed with Trouble while I picked up Craig and Roger. They'd shed their western attire for Margaritaville duds, shades and boat shoes. Both looked healthy and happy. It was too bad I was about to rain on their vacation.

Once we were all in the car, I said, "Uh, Craig, your mom called me today."

"She did?"

"Yep. When did you last speak with her?"

"Right after I...we...decided to come down here. Thought it was a good idea to let her know I was going out of the country on vacation. Why?"

"Because she and your dad are headed for La Paz to surprise you."

Craig and Roger chorused, "Oh, hell."

When we arrived at the boat, Craig examined Trouble and deemed our warm bath did a good enough job removing whatever the mess was all over him.

"Good. Sooo, what's the plan, guys?" I asked as we relaxed with cocolocos on deck.

"Just keep him warm. I'll take a blood sample tomorrow and send it to a lab. Also, I'll have one of those gooey feathers you saved tested to see if they can figure out what it was."

I looked at him under my eyebrows, "Craig, I mean about your parents. They'll be here tomorrow."

He and Roger exchanged a glance. Roger said, "You know we decided not to drop our relationship on our elderly parents. All four of them would be extremely distraught to learn their only sons are fairies."

"Oh, come on," Jan said. "Surely in this day and age—"

"Trust us," Craig said. "It's something we've agreed on. My parents have come to terms with their baby boy being what they call a confirmed bachelor, as have Roger's. We are content with each other, and don't find it necessary to upset the fruit cart, so to speak."

Chapter Five

CRAIG'S QUIP ABOUT upsetting his parents' fruit cart set all of us giggling, even Trouble. His laugh was usually a loud, "Haw haw haw," but in his weakened state, it was more of a, "Hee hee hee." When he said "fruit" at the end, that was a side-splitter.

After we calmed down, Craig said, "Roger's parents have been to the ranch, but since we maintain separate houses, it wasn't an issue. We got along really well. My folks have never been to Arizona, so they haven't even met Roger yet."

"Sounds stressful to me," I said, "but it's your lives. Anyhow, as you saw, the condo has two bedrooms, so you'll have separate closets, so to speak."

"Enough with the lame gay humor, okay?" Jan said, after a snort. "My stomach hurts."

"My stomach is growling. Let's go get some chow. I'll collect my badly-behaved hound and then you guys can haul him home with you after we eat."

When I coaxed Trouble into his cage, he weakly protested instead of raising the roof like he normally does until I wrestle him in and get a cover over the cage. He was already sawing logs as we left. Or, in his case, maybe dreaming of shredding Po Thang's ears.

Po Thang, whose ear was healing quickly from their run-in, was overjoyed to see Craig and Jan. He gave Roger, whom he'd never met, a friendly lick, and snubbed me. As we passed my boat, he strained on his leash and growled. I gave his lead a gentle jerk. "Give it a rest, Po. You two are gonna have to get over yourselves, but for now, *you* are the banned one. Suck it up, Buttercup."

Growl.

"Okay, bad boy, you asked for it. Jan, why don't you grab Trouble and take him with us. That okay, Craig?"

"Did you find his tether?"

"Unearthed it this morning before everyone arrived. It's behind his cage."

Jan and Craig returned with an energized Trouble. He knew he was going on an outing the minute they strapped him in his harness. He gave Po Thang a hiss and a wing flap. "Ack! Bad Dog!"

Po Thang went bonkers, but I had harnessed him, as well. Roger had his leash, so there was no way he was going anywhere. Just to make sure, I waved his hated muzzle in front of him as a threat. He settled down some, but nonetheless grumbled all the way to the Dock Café until he realized food was afoot. He quickly forgot about Trouble once we settled into our chairs and I let him loose to make the usual rounds of his adoring public with his, "*I am such a mistreated puppy. Please, oh, please may I have a morsel?*" act.

40

Trouble, on the other hand, promptly fell asleep.

While Po Thang successfully begged, we ordered drinks and four fresh snapper Veracruz dinners. As we waited for our food, I told Craig and Roger about our mysterious phone call, and the perceived cryptic signals, from Humberto, the man who was supposed to be taking care of Trouble.

Both frowned. Roger spoke first. "Sounds to me like he's tryin' to send you a message, alright. I've been livin' on the border all my life, and I'd bet a penny to a peso they had him call you back so's you don't come snooping 'round because that fella, Humberto, didn't return your calls. Too bad for them they're idiots who didn't pick up on his clues."

"And that now they are dealing with Hetta Coffey, to boot," Jan quipped.

"Yes, they are," I snarled. "I'm going to find out what happened to poor Trouble, and make someone pay for it."

Trouble, who was snoozing on Jan's shoulder, raised his head from under his wing and mumbled, "Poor Trouble." He sounded just like me, only...parrot-ier.

Roger growled "*We* will make them pay. Your posse is here now, and we for sure will hold some *zorillo's huevos* to the fire. There's nothin' that gets my dander up more than some skunk mistreating a helpless animal."

"Roger that, Roger."

He chuffed. "I get that a lot, Miz Hetta. Seems to me we need to take a foray out that way, and soon. Just whereabouts is this bird joint?"

Jan pulled her huge designer tote into her lap and handed Roger a map book of Baja. "Homework. I've folded over the corner of the page where Rancho Los Pajaros lies. It's circled in red."

I filled him in on the location and lay of the land. Jan added a few more details. "As you'll see, this map is very detailed. It shows almost every goat path, topographically."

Roger put on his glasses and gave the ranch's page a once over. "I'll mull on this later, but it looks to me at first glance like ideal horseback country. I'll make a few calls in the morning and come up with somethin'."

"Oh, hell," I groaned. "Just the *thought* of a cross-desert horseback ride makes my butt hurt and thighs ache. Craig was along the last time I rode a horse. It didn't turn out well."

"For her, or the horse," Craig said, and launched into what he considered a hilarious recount of me accidentally taking a horse tranquilizer for the ensuing pain from a day in the saddle.

My opinion of horseback riding is you should either do it all the time, or never.

Anything in between leads to excruciating misery for a gal.

My pickup, with its rear passenger jump seat, is not the most suitable vehicle for picking up two elderly, wealthy doctors from Atherton, California. Craig hired Rafael Taxi, who has a van and hangs out at Marina de la Paz.

While I fetched the "surprise" visitors, Jan and Craig

got bird duty, and Roger was saddled with Po Thang.

Craig's mother and father arrived dressed in natty vacation duds, something I'd never seen her wear. She was rarely dressed casually except for golf, which in Atherton, is a Ralph Lauren venue. Most of the time they were both attired in suits: she in Chanel and pearls, Armani for him.

I'd put on clean shorts and a tee shirt that wasn't stained or holey.

"Don't you look…relaxed, Hetta," Doctor Mother cooed. "Mexico must suit you."

Translation: *All you need is some gull shit on that dreadful hairdo.*

"Thanks, Doctor Washington. You're both looking spiffy."

Translation: *For a couple of old snobs.*

It was gonna be a looong week.

Once in the van, Doctor Mom said, "We were quite pleased to hear our son was coming to visit you. We've long since given up on grandchildren, but at least if you two…."

Translation: *I know you're far too old to have children, but you're better than nothing…*

She let that hang.

Oh, dear God! Call me up, now.

Unfortunately, the big man on high didn't get that mental text, so I was stuck. Not that I expected any favors from someone whose rules I break all too often.

Since this parental visit was supposed to be a big *coup de théâtre* for Craig, I delivered his parents straight to

Hotel La Perla on the *malecón* —La Paz's waterfront promenade. We conspired to have Craig and me meet them at the El Molokan restaurant at five. The owners are friends of mine; their son, Chef Roberto, got himself embroiled in a kidnapping scheme in Cannes, and I sorta bailed him out when we all got back to La Paz.

Okay, so I sorta shot a knife that was headed straight for his heart from the hand of a double-crossing woman he thought loved him. Her hand was a bit of a mess and required extensive reconstruction, but I considered her breakup method a tad on the harsh side, as well.

It is downright amazing how far I'll go to make friends with those who have first class food.

Thinking things might get a bit tense at this Craig/Roger/Mom/Dad dinner, I figured having friendly faces on the staff certainly wouldn't hurt.

Craig, Jan, Roger and I were cleverly seated boy, girl, boy, girl, at a round table set for six when the Doctors Washington, senior, arrived. We'd left two empty seats so the docs were sandwiched between Craig and Jan.

"Craig, here they come. Get ready to be surprised and delighted," Jan whispered.

He gave an academy-award-worthy double take when his folks entered, we all jumped to our feet, and he rushed to meet them. "Mother! Father! What on earth are you doing here?"

"We're here to see our only son, and his friends, dear boy. And Hetta helped set up our little surprise," his mother crowed.

"Well, I certainly *am* surprised and delighted. Come

sit down. I wondered who the two extra chairs were for."

His mother headed straight for Jan and gave her an air kiss. "You look lovely, as always, Jan. I wasn't aware you were here in La Paz. An added pleasure." She then turned her attention to Roger. "And you must be the famous Doctor Yee?"

"Oh, no," Jan said. "Doctor Yee, uh, Chino, couldn't be here this time of year…whales, you know. Actually, this is …"

Roger was already on his feet with his hand out. "Howdy. I'm Roger, Craig's partner."

I sucked in my cheeks.

Jan looked at Craig, eyes wide.

Craig opened his mouth to say something, but at that moment, Chef Roberto rushed from the kitchen, arms wide open. "Hetta! Jan! We are so pleased you could join us tonight!"

Dressed in full chef's garb, toque and all, he introduced himself to the older couple first, then there was a round of hellos, happy to meet yous, nice to meet y'alls and *mucho gustos*. "Please, please, sit. I must return to the kitchen to prepare you a special meal."

But first," he clapped his hands and a waiter materialized with menus. Roberto waved the menus aside, telling the waiter he was making the choices for the evening, and ordered our wine. As soon as he disappeared through the swinging doors we heard him shouting orders as pans and dishes clattered.

"My heavens," Doc Dad whispered, "I must say, I've never had the chef order my dinner before. I think I like it."

Mother Doctor looked skeptical. "I didn't realize Mexico *had* actual chefs."

Jan, never one to be out-snobbed, flicked her hair. "Oh, yes. He was chef on our yacht in Cannes last month. We trust him implicitly. He is excellent, right Hetta?"

Roger, who was just taking a sip of Margarita, choked and shot some out his nose. Three doctors stood to assist, but he waved them off. "I'm fine. Got something down the wrong tube."

Doc Mom gave him a look. "I'm sorry," she said, "exactly who did you say you were, again?"

"Mother, I've told you about Roger. We're partners in our ranch and large animal practice on both sides of the Arizona and Mexican border."

"You're a veterinarian, as well?" she asked Roger.

"No, ma'am. I'm just a rancher. I raise 'em, your son takes care of 'em."

"Roger is hardly *just* a rancher," I interjected. "His family has owned a huge spread on the Arizona border for five generations. His parents retired to Scottsdale and turned it all over to him a few years back."

Roger gave me an aww-shucks-ma'am grin. Craig visibly relaxed for the first time that evening after I steered, you should excuse the pun, the conversation toward ranching, Craig's innovations for tracking herds by GPS, and always a table winner: golf. Doc Father is an avid golfer, as is Roger, so they hit it right off and made a date to play.

We were running through wine like water, so by the time the steaming bowls of *Moules a la Roberto* arrived, we were all pretty uninhibited.

Chef Roberto's mussels steamed in white wine and hearty shrimp broth and enhanced with heavy cream, tequila, and small bits of spicy chorizo, was way up on my to-die-for list. And served in crockery bowls topped with thick slabs of toasted sourdough garlic bread for dunking? OMG! The plump shellfish, creamy and slightly spicy rich broth, and crunchy bread, helped soak up some of the alcohol we'd consumed.

"My goodness!" Mother Doc exclaimed, forgetting not to talk with her mouth full. "This is one of the best dishes I've ever tasted!"

That vote of approval alone made the whole evening worthwhile.

All we had to do now was get through another week without letting the eight-hundred- pound skeleton out of the armoire.

I know, mixed idioms.

Chapter Six

ON THE OFF-chance I'd been dead wrong about a problem at Rancho Los Pajaros, I tried calling Humberto again the next morning. His phone was, according to the message in Spanish, no longer in *servicio.*

That called for a war conference. When we were gathered on my aft deck, taking in the comings and goings of boats, dock workers polishing already shining yachts, and the occasional seal cruising the marina, I took a sip of much needed coffee and said, "Now I'm more worried about Humberto and Anna than ever. Their phone is no longer in service."

Jan shrugged. "You know that's not unusual in Mexico. If you are one day late paying your bill, they zap you. From the bird sanctuary it'd be an entire day spent driving into Loreto and paying their bill at the bank. And the lines at the bank can be incredibly time consuming."

"I know, but I don't believe in coincidence. I call, then the phone goes off line? *Zorillo* all over it."

"Ack! *Zorillo!*"

Jan grinned and gave Trouble a head scratch. "Hey,

pretty bird, do you know what happens when a skunk walks into a courtroom?"

Trouble shook his head, and Roger rolled his eyes. "I guess you're gonna tell us?"

"Odor! Odor in the court!"

Groans all around.

"Hadda do it. Anyhow, this phone thing does have a strong odor. I think you may be right. Hey, it happens."

"Getting your phone cut off for being only one day late?" Craig asked.

"Naw, Hetta being right."

"Hey, watch it. Anyone need more coffee? I'm going down for a refill. All that rich food and wine last night left mega cobwebs in my skull. Anyhow, I'm for driving up there tomorrow and taking a look at the sanctuary."

Roger shook his head. "You do need more head-clearing, Hetta. That might be a really bad idea."

"She's full of them," Jan quipped.

I gave her a cut-it-out glare.

"Roger," I insisted, "I *have* to know if Anna and Humberto are in danger. And how Trouble got into the shape he's in."

"I've been working on it," Roger said as he pulled out my map book, turned to the right page, and tapped on a location. "The ranch and bird sanctuary are about four miles past this here Mission San Javier, in the mountains west of Loreto, that right?"

"Yes, the road is paved as far as the mission, but after that, it's a crap shoot."

Jan nodded. "Hetta's right again. After hurricane

season, it's taken us a good hour or more to make that four miles, but usually it's a twenty minute drive, max. So from here to the ranch is a minimum of seven hours driving time, if we're lucky and don't get stuck behind too many slow trucks. We gonna pull an overnighter? I vote against it. Driving at night is a no-no."

Roger grinned. "You're pretty fast with the numbers, ain't ya, Blondie?"

I sucked in my breath. Jan hates being called Blondie and has a violent nature on occasion. I jumped in to prevent bloodshed. "She's a CPA, for cryin' out loud."

Evidently she didn't take offense at his nickname for her. I guess because it didn't come from a straight guy? "Yes, I'm a CPA, but old Blondie here has driven just about every godforsaken goat trail in Baja on Chino's so-called shortcuts. Hetta and I've weathered that last four miles from San Javier to visit Trouble many times, with varying results. We had a bad storm up there this year, so Lord only knows what we'll find. I vote we spend a night in Loreto and start out fresh the next morning."

I held up my index finger. "What *she* said."

Roger studied the map and shoved it over to me. "Okay then, I'll come up with a plan. When do you want to leave for Loreto?"

"Sooner the better. Hey, Craig, do we have to wait until the parents leave, or take them with us?"

Craig, who was returning from the galley with a fresh cup of coffee, evidently caught only the last part of the question. "Take who with us, and where?"

We laid out our plans for the run to Loreto and the

trek into the mountains. He mulled over the map for a minute, then tapped it with his finger. "Is that a resort I see?"

Jan and I exchanged a glance. "Uh, well, that might not be our best choice," Jan said. "Hetta is, like, *persona non grata* with those folks."

"Me? You're the one who dragged me there for a luau and beheading. And, by the way, signed into the hotel with *my* name."

"How was I to know Ishi was gonna lose his head?"

"Maybe not, but next time you sell yourself, you might consider getting the money up front. Who knows—"

"Ladies, ladies, please!" Roger held up his hands.

Jan and I whirled on him and yelled, in unison, "Don't call us ladies!"

That, of course, sent us into fits of laughter.

"Okay, okay, I can hardly wait to hear that whole story, but let's get back to the business at hand," Craig said. "You too, Trouble. Stop that giggling."

I swear, the bird sounded just like Jan and me when we got the giggles.

"As I was about to say, before you two got into a row, resorts appeal to Mother and Father."

Jan and I exchanged an eye roll at a grown man referring to his parents in such a formal manner, but then again, I'm a forty-year-old who still calls her father Daddy.

"I have a better suggestion. One that Hetta has not, to date, gotten us eighty-sixed out of, and it's closer to our ultimate destination. And, it's a resort, as well."

"Golf course?"

"Yep. It's just a tad south of Loreto, at a place called Nopolo. It's got swank, so your parents will love it. Think we'd be able to leave tomorrow? I have a bad feeling about what's going on at Rancho Los Pajaros."

Everyone agreed.

Jan headed for her computer, "I'll get on Airbnb's website. There are some spiffy digs at Loreto Bay Shores, and if we rent a really big house, the parents should be tolerable for two nights. Hey Rog, you and Craig want the bridal suite?"

There it was; Jan's revenge for the Blondie thing. I knew she couldn't let it slide.

After a few minutes on the computer, we agreed on a three-story, beachfront villa with three bedrooms. The Craig and Roger thing was easily dealt with; the third floor had a smallish bedroom with two twin beds. Jan and I would share the king on the second floor, and the parents got the master on the first floor. With Dad's wonky hip and Mom's fairly new knee replacement, they'd be confined to the downstairs area.

Craig took off for the hotel to meet his folks for breakfast and to discuss the excursion to Loreto, Roger headed for Rhonda's condo to arrange the trek to Rancho Los Pajaros, and Jan booked the villa in Loreto.

It was my job to figure out what to do with Trouble and Po Thang. I was leaning toward locking them in the boat together, and may the best man win.

Jan reminded me that my boat's interior could well be the loser.

We reassembled for a drink before meeting Craig's parents for dinner. The elder Doctors Washington insisted on eating at El Molokan every night, what with the charming Chef Roberto treating us like royalty.

I told everyone I'd arranged for my dock mate, Karen, to keep Po Thang again, and she would also drop in on Trouble several times a day to make sure he was eating and drinking. I was reluctant to leave him caged for that long, but Craig reminded me that: one; Trouble is a bird, and two; said bird needed to rest and recover. Hey, he's the vet.

Jan showed us photos of the villa she'd rented, and Craig agreed it was perfect and forwarded the info to his dad's email. He got an answer back almost immediately. They loved the idea of a trip and approved of the villa.

After Craig reported he'd managed to rent a van so we'd all fit, I said, "Okay, then. Roger, the rest is up to you."

"I got it handled. The mules will be ready when we get there on Wednesday morning."

"Mules? As in large stubborn beasts of burden?" I asked.

"Yep. Four of 'em, saddled and ready to go. Plus a guide. He figures round-trip about four hours once we get on the trail."

"That's quite a trek," Jan said.

"Yeah, like to Hell and back," I grumbled.

"Now, there's a place you might wanta warm up to, Hetta," she drawled. "But I wouldn't count on a round-trip, if I were you. Just sayin'."

I guffawed. I can always count on Jan for a yuk.

"Seriously, Roger, can't we just drive all the way?" Craig asked.

"Nope. I figgered it all out. Google Earth shows the enemy has the high ground. They'll see us comin' if we reconnoiter by road. We gotta envelop them from the rear so's we have the advantage."

I hid a smile. "Uh, let me guess, Roger. You were in the military?"

"You could say that. Border Patrol. Bein' practically born on horseback, that's what I did. Trackin'."

"I saw plenty of BP on horses when I rented that house near the Arizona border, but never a mule. One of the neighbors had some cute donkeys. I liked to listen to them honk in the morning. Remember them, Jan?"

"Yep, who could forget the daily wakeup call? However, Hetta, I believe the term is bray."

"Whatever. Why mules, Rog?"

"Border Patrol use rescued mustangs as a rule, but for mountainous areas, I'll take a mule any old day. Why do you think they use them at the Grand Canyon? Surefooted. And they don't spook. A horse'll shy away from somethin' scary. But a mule? He'll take it on. Stomp a rattlesnake all to hell. And a coyote, too. Also, mules often inherit the donkey *fight* response to danger instead of the horse's *flight* reaction. If a horse gets spooked, and isn't sure what it was that scared him, he'll usually run.

Which is a danged good way to throw a rider, or get both of 'em hurt."

"Been there, done that," I said.

He nodded. "Now you take a mule, he'll spin to face a perceived enemy. This gives him time to decide whether the threat is real or not. One thing this'll do is keep other mules or horses behind him from doin' something stupid. A lead horse who rabbits out of control on a trail ride can cause other animals to panic, as well. On a narrow mountain path, it can turn deadly."

"I remember my granddad kept donkeys on the ranch to run off coyotes. Did a fine job of it, too," I told him.

"And, Hetta, mules can handle more weight," Jan added.

I get no respect.

Chapter Seven

ONE OF THE things Roger failed to tell us was that from Loreto to the mule corral, he'd arranged for us to ride quads. I hate quads.

"We'll look less suspicious. What with helmets and all, if we get spotted after we pass San Javier, no one'll be able to tell who we are, male or female."

I gave Craig a once-over and brayed. "Yeah, the Baja abounds in six-foot-four, black women on quads. Nothin' to see there."

We decided on helmets with facemasks.

As we suspected—and counted on—the senior docs were not at all interested in joining us for a desert quad jaunt. I knew the feeling. It was about the last thing I wanted to do; right behind the mule train ride up a mountain. And back down.

We arranged a day tour of Loreto and Mission San Javier for the parents, and the rest of us were ready to take off at oh-dark-thirty for the nine-mile drive into Loreto.

The first stretch of mountainous, curvy road to Mission San Javier was paved, and gave me a chance to get used to my scary four-wheeled machine. After all, I didn't know squat about boats until I bought *Raymond Johnson*, and the quad had something my boat didn't— brakes. So, by the time we hit dirt, I was feeling more confident.

Because I am allergic to dust, Roger and I took the lead, with Jan and Craig dropping back to avoid our fallout which, luckily, an early morning breeze whisked away quickly. I rode slightly upwind of Roger, taking it slow over the surprisingly good road. Someone was grading it, and it was in the best condition we'd ever seen. Amazing what a little cartel money can do when smugglers need to move their product quickly.

When we turned off the main road, I was thankful the last few kilometers to the mule corral were not as bad as I'd feared. However, by the time we reached the tree-shaded, almost bucolic spread, I realized how tensed up I'd been on the quad. My shoulders and arms ached, my ears rang from the motor noise, and I was almost looking forward to ditching the machine for a nice, quiet, mule. Almost.

Jan's eyes widened when we met the mules kinner. We'd both expected a wizened old cowboy who smelled like his mules.

The tall, fortyish and handsome man dressed in perfectly fitting jeans, slightly scuffed but good quality boots, and a Stetson, stuck out his hand. "Welcome to Camp Muleshoe. I'm Drew Campanella, your host for the day."

Jan tittered like a teen. "I get it, Campanella…Camp. Very clever. You're American?"

I mentally rolled my eyes. Gawd, she's easy. But I had to admit, he was a hunk. Blue eyes in a tanned face, blondish hair from what I could see from the long fringe on his neck. Determined not to seem like I was fazed by his movie star looks, I said, all business-like, "Hetta Coffey here. Nice to meet you, Drew. Great place. An oasis in the middle of desolation. You must have a good well."

"I do, and I have an elaborate water catchment system for the rainy season. The main house has been here since the eighteen hundreds, but I did some improvements."

My immediate thought was, *trust-fund baby.* The Baja is full of them. Nodding my head toward the well-maintained barn and corral, I asked, "Which one is mine?"

Drew pointed to the largest mule in the pen. The brute looked…mulish. When I said as much, Jan retorted, "It takes one to tell one. Let me count the ways. As in, obstinate, stubborn, pigheaded, recalcitrant, intransigent, unyielding, inflexible, and bullheaded. Sound like anyone we know, guys?"

"How long have you been harboring that Thesaurus hack to insult me with, Miz Jan?"

"Some time now, Chica. It was a certainty the opportunity would arise."

"You gotta get a life up there at that whale camp. You have *way* too much time on your hands in between flipping tortillas."

"Hey, you two, let's get going, okay?" Craig said.

I sized up my ride. Huge. And cross-eyed. I swear when he saw me he rolled his eyes in opposite directions, which showed a lot of white. White-eye on a horse ain't a good sign, but our *transportador de mulas*, assured me Hedley was a grand mount, just a little pie-eyed.

Hedley's broad back at first seemed like a plus, but my inner thighs soon screamed that riding in a constant plié position is far from ideal.

Mule skinner Drew led us out of camp, onto a well-traveled path toward a steep upgrade, which I glared at with dread. To take my mind off my already blazing inner thighs, and quite frankly, some of my more delicate bits, I asked, "Say, Roger, when you told us about this foray, you used the words 'envelop them from the rear flank.' Does envelop mean *attack*? Ride down for vengeance like Cochise did from his mountain stronghold to rob and pillage settlers and soldiers?"

I'd visited Cochise's stronghold in the Chiricahua Mountains of Arizona, and it was obvious that the Indian leader could spot anyone for miles around from his high spot.

Jan laughed from atop her svelte mule. "Cochise rode mules? Sounds like a Mel Brooks movie." I noticed her thighs comfortably hugged her skinny-assed mule, and her elongated stirrups kept her legs only slightly bent. I had stirrup envy.

"Nah," I said, "he rode mustangs. Right Roger?

Roger nodded.

"But speaking of Mel Brooks? Hello, my critter is named Hedley. What do you bet his last name is Lamarr?"

This prompted a rash of Blazing Saddles quotes.

"Hey, Craig, 'they said you was hung'."

Craig countered, "'And they was right.'"

Roger said, in a high voice, " 'Oh, it's twue. It's twue. It's twue, it's twue'!"

We all laughed, then our guide warned us, "The sound. It carries a long way up here."

"Yes, Kemosabe," I whispered.

Roger lowered his own voice. "As for Cochise, I have a story to tell."

"We're all ears, right Hedley?" I reached forward and fondled my mule's fuzzy ear, and he groaned with pleasure. I think. I braced myself for an odiferous mule fart, just in case.

"Ya see, old Cochise had hisself a deal with the US government to protect the stage coach line, but there was a major foul-up when a new guy with no Indian experience ended up holding him responsible for a raid on a ranch, and the kidnapping of the rancher's twelve-year-old son."

"Lemme guess. He didn't do it?" Jan said.

"Nope, it was another band of Apaches, but that Lt. Bascom didn't know one Indian from 'tother, so they arrested Cochise. He escaped by cutting a hole in the back of a tent, then Bascom retaliated by taking some of his relatives, then Cochise took hostages, and both sides ended up killin' their captives."

"That'd have a way of souring their deal," Craig said.

"Big time. Ended up in an eleven-year war with estimates as high as five-thousand killed. That might be an exaggerated number, but it was still a big mess."

"And," I asked, "wasn't there a bunch of gold involved somehow?"

Jan grinned. "Gold is Hetta's favorite subject."

I shrugged, "And why not?"

Craig chuckled. "Roger's spent years searching every cave, crook, and cranny in Cochise County looking for that stash. We'll show you the maps he made when you come to Arizona."

Jan narrowed her eyes at me. "Hetta, you've gone as pie-eyed as your mule. Forget about the gold."

Jan's warning to give up on the idea of a gold hunt in Arizona fell on deaf ears, for at least dreams of riches distracted me somewhat from my searing thigh muscles. I'd resorted to balancing cross-legged in the saddle to relieve my overstretched thighs.

Our guide rode forward, held up his arm, and whistled. Hedley heard the signal, came to an abrupt halt, and I ended up hanging sideways on my mount. Only my death grip on the saddle horn kept me from falling on my head.

I'd managed to swing both legs onto terra firma in what I considered a rather elegant save when Roger said, "Dismount."

"Hetta already beat us to it," Jan said dryly.

We gathered our backpacks, cameras, canteens, and

binoculars and set off on foot. Not much of a hiker, I nevertheless reveled in being on my own two feet and stretching my legs. At least for about five minutes, when I panted, "How...far...do we have to go?"

"Less than a kilometer; maybe nine hundred meters," Drew told us.

I looked up—way up—and gasped, "Piece of cake," but I wanted my mule back.

Chapter Eight

AFTER AN ALMOST vertical climb, I brought up the rear to find my friends already lying on the edge of a drop-off, checking out the flatland below. When I finally caught a breath, I joined them and immediately recognized the farmhouse and bird enclosure below, but something was off. It took me a moment to realize what. Only native bird sounds surrounded us. No exotic squawks.

"About time you dragged yourself up here," Jan whispered.

"Bite me," I wheezed.

"I'm cutting excess fat from my diet. You see what I see?" she asked.

"I know what I hear. *Nada.*"

She nodded and handed me her binoculars. "Check out the farmhouse."

I adjusted the Bushnells to my vision—miffed she could see better than me—and zeroed in on two guys in hoodies with what looked to be automatic weapons slung over their shoulders. They were chatting and smoking. I trained on the bird enclosure; there were a few birds in it, but they looked to be natives that habitually sneaked in for a free meal. They were quietly huddled together against the cool morning.

"Humberto always covers part of the aviary so the birds can shelter from rain, cold and sun. His canvas is nothing but tatters now. I—"

"Shhhh," Roger said. "I hear something. Sounds like a truck."

Sure enough, a bright yellow truck resembling a Mexican roach coach crested a small rise in the road, sounded the well-known ballad, "La Cucaracha," on his horn, then rumbled through the gate when the armed men opened it. It stopped briefly at the main house, then followed the guards to the aviary.

Although the truck's gaily painted sides boasted the best tacos in all of Mexico, it had been modified. Unlike a typical street diner, the rear had a roll-up canvas. Once it was open, the driver began lugging boxes inside the bird enclosure through a man door. Okay, *person* door. Sheesh.

The few birds already inside flew around nervously, one actually escaping right over the heads of the men. "You go, bird," I whispered under my breath.

Jan gave me a double thumbs-up.

It took a good twenty minutes to get all the cardboard boxes inside the enclosure and shut the door. The man doing all the work then began unsealing his cargo, revealing fruit of all kinds: mangos, papaya, melons, and pineapple. When about half the boxes were open, he started removing the tops of the others.

"*¡Pendejos!*" Roger spat under his breath.

I adjusted my binocular lenses, as we all did, and watched a large, bedraggled parrot slowly pull himself out by his beak. As he did so, his weight tipped the box, and three more birds staggered out into the morning light.

Craig whistled. "Holy crap! Those are hyacinth macaws! They retail in the US for thousands of dollars." He whipped out our best video camera and recorded the disturbing scene as at least two hundred brilliantly colored exotic birds—blinking and panting while staggering in their pigeon-toed manner—succeeded in leaving their box-prisons. Only one box remained still, and I watched it until it finally began to jiggle. I breathed a sigh of relief that something was still alive in there.

We gave each other updates; I was zeroed in on the confused, loose birds, as one by one, they stumbled toward a large water trough which, thank God, someone had filled. So far, the piles of fruit were only of interest to the indigenous birds. Swallows, orioles, and doves that had sneaked in for a fast meal were now trapped but got their reward of fruit.

I sighed. "At least now they all have food and water."

"Yabbut," Jan said, "only one big blue macaw is nibbling on the fruit. The rest are still dazed, but at least they're drinking water like Hetta guzzles beer."

I nudged her in the ribs. "That's the ultimate pot calling the kettle black."

We high-fived.

Roger, who was too engrossed with the scene below to appreciate our juvenile antics, growled. "Those a-holes'll get 'em fed, rested up and ready to move again, so's to get the best bang for their buck up north."

Craig nodded and let loose a couple of expletives, himself. "Then they get them across any way they can. Birds are drugged, stuffed in pipes, covered in cooking oil, and crammed into empty plastic water bottles, which is what I suspect happened to Trouble. I read somewhere customs arrested a guy at some airport with six of the poor birds strapped to his legs. These guys down there? Looks like the fruit was in the back of the truck to hide the real cargo through any Mexican military inspection posts."

Our guide, Drew, who had been fairly quiet up until now added, "And there were, of course, pesos exchanging hands. The military here, even the officers, don't make much money. If they work with the cartels while in *servicio,* they'll be rewarded well."

I'd heard the cartels were recruiting trained soldiers into their ranks, offering amounts beyond most Mexicans' dreams. My binocs were trained on the one box that so far remained intact when a head popped up; a bird struggled out and toppled onto the ground, followed by six more. Even I could identify this flock, as a friend of mine has owned one for many years. I pointed to them. "Yellow-headed Amazons."

Roger swung his binoculars and watched the birds waddle in circles. "Those bastards! Double yellows are on the endangered species list. Worse than that, even; they're facing extinction. Poor things have been dosed with something to keep them silent and immobile. Most likely cheap tequila or aguardiente."

"Ick," I said, remembering when I tasted the vile booze. "That stuff comes in gallon jugs. Aguardiente is the white lightning of Mexico. You can both drink it and use it for lantern fuel."

Roger looked grim. "The smugglers force it down their throats, then hold their beaks until they swallow. Poor little guys are still drunk. They're lucky to still be breathing."

"So that's how they get them across the border?" I asked, trying to envision a truckload of squawking birds crossing through the US entry in California. I'd sat in that line for up to three hours a few times.

"Yep. They knock them out to keep them quiet. No telling how far these birds have traveled, and a load of noisy, illegal, birds isn't something you want to draw attention to. I wonder how many dead ones are still in those boxes."

My stomach did a turn, then bottomed out when one of the gunmen suddenly stopped and stared intently in our direction. "Crap!"

Drew saw him, as well. "Fast! Cover your cameras and binoculars. The sun is reflecting off of them this time of day. Give it a few minutes and we'll be good again."

We did as we were told, but I wondered if he had been up here recently, and if he saw anything. However, in Mexico it is never a good idea to ask too many questions when you require someone's help. I showed him a small pair of plastic binoculars my dad gave me. Not very strong, but okay. They were solid black with no metal to reflect light. I showed them to Drew and he nodded but indicated that I not point them into the sunlight.

Very slowly, from behind a boulder, I sneaked a peek. The man below still stared up in our direction, probably trying to decide if he'd actually seen a flash of light or heard something. After a minute or so—I didn't know I could hold my breath that long—he shouldered his weapon and sauntered toward the house. "He's lost interest," I reported.

"Okay, rangers, pack up and let's get ready to ride," Roger said, twirling his index finger. "We've seen enough of this crap."

"We're just gonna leave those poor birds like this?" Jan protested.

"Miz Jan, what do you want us to do? They have automatic weapons."

"Yabbut, Hetta, at least you have a—"

I jabbed her in the side with my little binoculars to silence her before she blurted out that I was packing.

She yelped in protest and Roger, misunderstanding her outburst, patted her shoulder. "They'll be fine for now. Those bastards have to get the birds a whole lot healthier before they ship them out again. Not that they care about the birds. But dead birds are worthless. Anyhow, there's nothing we can do right this minute unless you want to ride in like the Charge of the Light Brigade and get our asses shot off. When we return, things'll be a *lot* more even."

Craig agreed. "It'll take at least a week to ten days to get those poor birds back in any shape for another trip.

Not all of them are as resilient as Trouble. Keep your fingers crossed we don't get a cold snap before we can rescue them. They're from the tropics, and most will die without a warm shelter. We can only hope those idiots down there know that. After all, they can't sell a sick or dead bird."

Jan and I reluctantly assented to leave, and basically butt-slid back down the cliff to our mules. It took me two tries and every expletive I knew in at least three languages before I finally launched my leg far enough across that fat-backed beast and hefted myself into the saddle.

I was *not* amused, but Jan sure was.

During the ride down the mountain, I was once again grateful for Hedley's surefootedness. Drew, who took pity on me and tied a double folded thick blanket across my saddle, led the way down at a slow pace, and that buffer he'd placed between my rear and the leather, to ease what my British riding friends called chuff chaff. That gave me a chance to relax a little and enjoy the ride. Unfortunately, once we hit flat land our mounts picked up the pace.

Suffice it to say that a mule in a hurry to get back to ye olde *ramada* has more bounce to the ounce.

Chapter Nine

AS IF ATV and mule riding hadn't put a serious enough hitch in my gitalong, I was so worried about Trouble that my stomach was in an uproar. I pestered my dog-and-parrot sitter, Karen, for updates, even though Craig assured me his being caged and alone for a short time would be therapeutic and gave him quiet time to heal. However, after witnessing the ordeal he probably went through, I couldn't help but fret. A mental picture of him drugged and stuffed into a water bottle set my teeth on edge. *Some*one was going to pay dearly for this.

On the drive back to our rental house at Loreto Bay, I called my dockmate once again. Karen, much to my relief, reported Trouble slept most of the day, and was now eating everything she gave him.

She also said Po Thang was being a very good boy.

I actually believed the part about Trouble.

Mom and Pop Doc, enthralled with not only the rental house, but the upscale, mostly Gringo neighborhood of Loreto Shores, and the nearby charming town of Loreto, decided to stay another day or two.

There was no way I could wait any longer to get back home, unless we were going to actually *do* something about the birds. My own critters in La Paz needed my attention and lollygagging around a resort was not in the cards.

Roger, probably relishing time alone with Craig without his parents, quickly arranged a car and driver to return the seniors Washington to la Paz in a few days, just in case they changed their minds about staying before we got out of town. He even paid for the house.

It took two Extra Strength Advil PM's to finally put me to sleep, despite being dog tired. I simply couldn't wipe the vision of those unfortunate birds, and those *pendejos* with guns, from my already overtaxed brain.

I ran into Jan in the kitchen around midnight. She, too, was downing a sleeping aid.

"Can't sleep either, huh?" she asked as she finished off a bottle of water. She'd been watching a movie downstairs when I went to bed.

"I want to kill someone."

"Oh, you'll get your chance. I was just thinking it's kinda nice to have an enemy no one will miss if we drop them in a well."

"Ooooh, now I think I can sleep. Thanks, Miss Jan, for something lovely to dream about."

I returned to my bed and went comatose, like Po Thang after a day at the beach.

Ah, the sweet dreams of mayhem.

We left Loreto very early the next morning. Roger was

eager to get gone before Mom and Pop even got their coffee. Our first stop in La Paz was at the marina so I could check on Trouble, while Jan collected Po Thang for a walk before dropping him off at the condo with Craig and Roger.

I managed, with a great deal of pain, to exit the van, then executed an awkward cowboy swagger/hustle down the dock, anxious to see my parrot, stretch out on a soft couch, and pop a beer cap, not necessarily in that order.

Trouble broke into a rendition of "The Yellow Rose of Texas" when he saw me, but not in his normal robust manner; the one that fries ear hair.

Letting him out of his cage, I grabbed an ice cold Tecate, sank onto my oh-so-cushy settee, and took a swig. The phone barked, Trouble squawked—probably thinking that evil varmint, Po Thang, had returned—and flew back into his jail for protection. I had to change that ring tone.

I checked caller ID and smiled. "Hi there, sailor boy. New in town? Wanna buy me a drink?"

"I sure would like to, sea wench, but I have to work."

"Well, hell, Jenks, guess I'll have to drink alone. How's Dubai?"

"Sizzling outside. Freezing in the house. My host keeps the thermostat at fifty-five."

"Why?"

"Because he can?"

I chuckled. "Saudi princes can pretty much do what they want. He still mad at me?"

"Naw, he never really was. Gave him a chance to redecorate, but you have to admit, you were a little rough on his yacht."

I huffed indignantly. "Well then, I certainly hope he redecorates his arsenal, as well. If I'd had a couple surface to air missiles on board when I was trying to outrun the bad guys in the Med, his boat would have fared much better. Let that be a lesson for him."

Jenks couldn't stifle a chuckle. "Hetta, you crack me up. I am constantly amazed how you manage to justify the damage you leave behind when called to action. I'll relate that bit of convoluted reasoning to him. It will make his day."

I realized how ridiculous my retort might sound to most sane people, and we laughed together, then talked a bit about my little adventure in the south of France: the one that left me with a new friend here in Baja, Chef Roberto.

Finally he asked, "Where were you yesterday? I tried to call a couple of times."

"Damned Telcel. Probably out of range. Did you leave a message?"

"No. They said you were not in *servicio*."

"Roger and Craig and Hetta and Jan went on a mission."

"Dare I ask where, and why?"

I told him about the trip to Loreto, complained about the quads, mule ride, and my resulting pain. Then I reported what we saw at Rancho Los Pajaros, my fears for Humberto and Anna, and what had probably happened to poor Trouble. At the mention of his name, he flew back to land on my shoulder.

"¡*Pendejos!*" Jenks said, loud enough for Trouble to hear and repeat.

"Put a lid on it, bird. You're busting my ear drums. And Jenks, that's exactly what Roger called these lowlifes."

"Great minds, and all. But I have a question. Trouble is hardly what you'd call an exotic bird, so why would they risk smuggling him into the US? There are those in the States who would *pay* someone to round them up and take them to Mexico."

It was an excellent question, one Jan and I had mulled over. Leave it to Jenks to go right for the obvious. He came to the same conclusion we had: some A-hole without much knowledge of birds grabbed Trouble, drugged him, stuffed him in a bottle, was informed he wasn't worth squat, and tossed the bottle away. Somehow, Trouble had escaped. The whole thing made me sick and mad.

Just as I was saying goodbye to Jenks, Jan showed up and yelled, "Howdy, Jenks," loud enough so he could hear her.

Ending my call, I told her what Jenks said about Trouble maybe being treated like trash because he was of no value. "¡*Pendejos!*"

"Yep, that pretty much makes it unanimous."

"And we gotta get 'em."

"Yes. We. Do."

I was hot to trot to return to the scene of the bird crimes, but Roger assured me he had Drew the muleteer on top of the situation, and he was going to get daily reports on the happenings up there. Besides, we were facing a few more days with the senior doctors Washington when they returned from Loreto.

Roger played golf with Doctor Dad, Craig went off to a meeting with local veterinarians concerning Trouble's health, and to learn more about the bird trafficking, while Jan and I were stuck with Madam Doc. I worried we got the hardest job of the day; that woman ain't easy to entertain.

"Whaddya think about taking her on a tour of Todos Santos, and maybe Costco in Cabo?" Jan suggested.

"I can't quite picture her at Costco, but Todos Santos? Great idea. We can do the loop of the east cape. What with lunch, it'll take all day. Only leaves two more. Not that I'm counting, of course."

Belgian weavers must have gone into overtime when Mother Washington ordered her vacation wardrobe. I was building up to a bad case of linen envy.

"Dang, she looks good for someone her age," Jan whispered under her breath as we walked toward her table where she waited for us at Hotel La Perla. "Hey, if you married Craig like his mom wants, lost fifty pounds, and then she kicked the bucket, would you get her clothes?"

"That's…ridiculous, but funny. But come on, fifty?—Good morning, Doctor Washington."

"Hetta, dear, perhaps you should call me Martha. And you, as well, Jan, since we're all practically family now."

Jan bit her lip at that *now* implication. "I'll go get our ride." When she turned her back to the doc, she mouthed at me, "Martha Washington? Are you freaking kidding me?"

Martha chatted non-stop, practically planning her son's—in her mind—dream wedding to me! "You must allow plenty of time, when you two pick a date, to get up to the city so we can choose your gown. I think perhaps off-white? Oh, and new wardrobe. Those shorts and tee shirts simply must go. And then, of course, Doctor Washington and I will accompany you on a 'round the world cruise. Don't you think that's grand?"

Hmmm. It was almost tempting. All that linen!

I was contemplating, however, informing the delusional woman that not only would it not be so grand, since I wouldn't be marrying her son anytime soon, and even if I did, horning in on his honeymoon was a terrible idea. I was saved that task by Jan rounding the corner in her Jeep and screeching to a halt in front of the hotel. Po Thang was sitting in the passenger seat.

My future mother-in-law's jaw dropped. "There's no top on that…whatever it is."

"We removed the canvas so you can enjoy the view. You'll be needing this." Jan handed her a baseball cap with I HEART BAJA embroidered on it.

"Po Thang," I said, "get your furry ass into the back seat with me."

Mom Doc tsked. "Language, dear."

I climbed in with Po Thang while Craig's mother pulled a hankie—linen, of course—from her Coach bag and draped it over her seat. I'd already brushed off dawg debris, but she was taking no chances.

"Hoookay, welcome to Hetta and Jan's tour service. We have a great day planned for you, Martha, but I think we need a jumpstart." Leaving the Jeep idling, Jan headed for the hotel and soon returned with a waiter in tow. On a silver platter sat three gigantic Bloody Mary's to go. By the time we got to Todos Santos, Mom was happy as a clamato and vodka. Jan later told me she ordered a Virgin Mary for herself but made Mom's a double.

After a Mexican breakfast for four in Todos Santos, more Bloody Marys, and a walking tour of the artsy town, we turned south for Cabo San Lucas. Wandering through shops and accepting free Margaritas from timeshare salesmen, we left Cabo and drove to the east cape of the Baja peninsula, passing gorgeous beaches, the Tropic of Cancer, and vistas fit for travel brochures.

In Los Barriles we enjoyed a latish lunch of fresh lobster, and more Margaritas. We had some difficulty steering Mom away from a real estate office where she was prepared to whip out her checkbook and buy a beach home for Craig and me as a wedding present.

By the time we reached La Perla in La Paz, it was happy hour. Roger, Craig, and Dad Doc were waiting for us at the hotel's patio restaurant.

I steadied Mother Washington as she toddled out of the Jeep and weaved toward the men. Her café au lait complexion was a shade rosy, her designer sunglasses were askew, and she had hat hair on one side of her head. "Oh, my, we had such a wonderful day! Hetta is a delightful hostess! She'll be a grand addition to the family."

The men's heads tipped in confusion like a litter of quizzical puppies.

Jan, trying to make light of Mom's statement, jested, "Hey, I did all the driving. Does that get me in the will?"

Po Thang, eager to get to Craig—and the plate of tapas in front of him—accidentally (I think) bumped into Craig's mom, and she almost took a header. I dove in for the save.

"Damned cobblestones," she said with a giggle when I righted her.

"Martha!" I admonished. "Language!"

She giggled, and Craig rushed forward to help his mother and steered her to a chair. Once she was safely seated, he turned to me and whispered, "What have you done to my mother? I love it. But what's this thing about you being an addition to the family?"

I jerked my head toward the jeep and said, "Give me a hand with your mother's packages, okay?"

When we were out of hearing range of the group around the table, I shook my head in mock sadness and sighed. "The groom is always the last to know. We're getting married, and your parents are gonna take us on a world cruise for the honeymoon."

"What? How much have you women had to drink today?"

"Not enough. I'll fill you in later."

While we ordered drinks—Jan and I had cleverly switched to virgin *everything* earlier in the day—Roger and Craig's dad recounted, ad nauseum, their day on the golf course hole by hole. It made me miss Jenks, who didn't remember squat most of the time, but could recount a game from a year ago in great detail.

We listened politely until the golfers finally reached the eighteenth hole. Dad won, and Roger gracefully acknowledged the senior man's golf prowess before changing the subject to Trouble by asking Craig for an update of his day.

"One of the local vets I met with today followed me to the boat, took a look at Trouble, and pretty much confirmed what we suspected. Our little bird was most likely drugged, slathered in veggie oil, and stuffed into a container for shipment.

"Wait! Trouble let the veterinarian examine him?"

"Not hardly. I liked the man too much to let Trouble loose on him. The vet just wanted a good look at our little survivor. After he received the blood-and-feather-goo test results confirming traces of Tequila and lard, he was amazed Trouble was able to fly to safety. He says the little guy looks good to him and once he regrows a few feathers and completely recovers from his hangover, he should be back to normal."

Po Thang growled.

Jan huffed. "Lawdy Maudy, help us."

I added, "Not sure that's such good news, but thank goodness for it, anyhow."

"So now," Doc Mom said, loud enough to be heard throughout the restaurant, "we can turn our attention to offing off those *pendejos* who hurt him!"

A nearby waiter almost dropped his tray of dishes.

Chapter Ten

WITH THE HUNKY mule wrangler, Drew, on Roger's payroll, I was able to relax some about the situation at Rancho Los Pajaros. He made the trek to our lookout each day, texted in a report with copies to me, Jan, and Roger, and sometimes sent photos. He didn't have the sophisticated equipment we'd used when we were up there, but at least the bird's-eye pics let us know nothing major had changed.

The "taco" truck we'd seen on our trip arrived on occasion, but Drew told us only fruit and supplies were offloaded. He tried taking a video for us with his phone, but it was grainy and almost useless. The one thing that had me stewing was that he still hadn't caught sight of Humberto and Anna, so I called each day to check their phone, but it remained out of service.

Drew also reported that, as far as he could tell, the birds were being well fed and seemed on the mend, judging by the cacophony of normal parrot noises blowing in on the morning breezes. And I was relieved to read that a tarp had been stretched over one end of the enclosure's roof, and what looked like solar heaters were installed. At least the *pendejos* appreciated the worth of their captives enough to protect them from a January cold snap.

Jan and I scoured the web, searching for clues from exotic bird-smuggling busts as to when and how the *pendejos*, as they were now permanently dubbed, might attempt to move the birds to another location in Mexico, or directly smuggle them across the border into the US. Historically, the record showed the birds are captured in southern Mexico, and even South American countries, and then first shipped somewhere in northern Mexico before making the final journey into the States.

Roger relayed all the information we garnered from Drew directly to the US Customs and Border Patrol via an old pal who still worked with homeland security, but we were still trying to decide *our* next move. Raid Rancho Los Pajaros? Jan and I were for storming in with guns blazing, but Roger cautioned against such a rash move without extensive backup. Oh, and guns. He didn't know I had my .380 on the boat, and anyhow, up against the *pendejos'* automatic weapons it was well-nigh useless.

While waiting to take action, I was in the throes of making peace reign on my boat. Po Thang was now allowed to visit for a couple of hours each morning, but I still caged Trouble while he was on board. They squawked, barked and generally grumbled their distaste for each other, letting me know they were in no way interested in détente. I had to do something fast, as all my compadres were making plans to leave me alone with the battling duo.

Mom and Pop Washington departed with no further mention of the upcoming nuptials. I had the impression Pop had put a lid on Mom, much to Craig and Roger's relief. However, I told them they needed to get that mess straightened out with the parents for everyone's sake.

But then again...all that linen!

Craig declared Trouble had recovered enough to defend himself, and I missed having Po Thang on board, so the day before Craig and Roger left for Arizona to tend to much-needed home chores, I decided to let the best pet win.

Collecting Po Thang from the condo, I took him for a long walk and when we returned to the boat, I opened Trouble's cage door. He slowly exited in his pigeon-toed way, all the while keeping a wary eye on the devil dog. He climbed to the top of his enclosure, out of dog's reach. He fluffed his now oil-free feathers to make himself look larger, hissed a couple of times in Po Thang's direction, then mumbled a string of expletives in both Spanish and English.

Holding tight onto Po Thang's collar, I gave Trouble a large piece of Oh, Boy! Oberto teriyaki turkey jerky, and Po Thang a Beggin' Strip. Trouble took the jerky in his beak, flew to the top of the steering station—still just out of Po Thang's reach—and nibbled, never once taking one eye off his foe.

Po Thang, torn for a moment between trying to eat the bird or settling for his bacon-flavored goody, swallowed the treat whole and *then* made an ineffective lunge toward Trouble.

Although perched much too high for Po Thang to grab, Trouble was so startled by the snarling beast from hell trying to attack him, he dropped his jerky.

Po Thang went in for the steal, gobbled it down and then sat quietly, looking to Trouble for seconds. I gave the parrot another piece, he broke it in half, and dropped the other piece to the waiting Po Thang.

An entire bag of jerky later, I was slouched on my settee. Trouble slept on my shoulder, and Po Thang was cuddled up against my leg, sound asleep himself.

Voilà! The Jerky Accords!

Exhausted by all the bird and dog drama, I also drifted off and awoke to Jan taking a photo of the three of us. She checked her phone screen and held it up for me to see. I made a grab for it, dislodging both animals in my determination to delete what was surely an unflattering shot of me snoring, mouth wide open.

Jan jerked the phone away and said, "Oh, no you don't, Chica. This is Facebook-worthy."

"I'll be the judge of that," I snarled. Jan and I had a deal not to post stuff of each other without prior approval.

"Come on, Chica," she showed it to me, "it's sweet."

I had to admit she was right. My mouth was shut, no drool rolled down my chin, and I had a contented smile on my face. Trouble was cute, leaning up against my neck, and Po Thang was sweetly grinning in his sleep, his chin on my leg.

"Okay, you can post it. So, Auntie Jan, how do you like this bonding thing?"

She sat next to Po Thang and rubbed his ears. He opened one eye and then went back to snoozing, but Trouble, evidently still not totally convinced that Po Thang wasn't the devil's spawn, climbed onto my head, and then hopped on Jan's for higher ground.

"How did you manage such a miracle, Hetta?"

"I sacrificed my very last bag of Oh! Boy! Oberto turkey jerky."

Trouble squawked, "Oh! Boy! Oberto!"

Po Thang sat up, looked around, and gave the bird a squint-eye. It was returned, and I said, "Brace yourself, Jan. The peace accords could very well go south any second now."

Jan and I prepared to move out of harm's way but, amazingly, the two former adversaries decided to ignore each other. We called Roger and Craig over to the boat to witness the *milagro* and to hold a powwow about our next step in dealing with the Rancho Los Pajaros situation.

And maybe Trouble's wings.

Although Craig was pleased with the way my animals were behaving toward each other, he vetoed a wing-clipping until he was positive Po Thang wasn't going to chomp on a bird that couldn't fly away.

"So, what you're saying is that any clipping will get done after you've fled to the safety of Arizona?" I accused.

"Absolutely. Do I look stupid?"

Trouble laughed his, "Haw, haw," and added, "stupid! Ack! Stupid!"

I certainly could not question Craig's sanity; I'd have to deal with grounding Trouble later, when both dog and bird alike proved trustworthy.

Meanwhile, back at the ranch (I've always wanted to say that), we had a more pressing problem looming. Roger and Craig were leaving, Jan couldn't stay much longer, and I was going to be left with only Drew spying on the aviary, and no new ideas of how to save the birds. "We can't just abandon them," I pleaded. "And I can't handle the situation alone."

"I'm not so sure of that," Craig said, "but we don't want you to. That's why we've been in touch with some authorities up north."

Jan nodded. "Good. And I'll only be a short drive away if I have to meet Hetta in Loreto. Even then, though, we need more manpower and a plan of action."

Craig grinned. "Jan, did you just say *man*power? I'm shocked."

Jan shot him a digit. "You know what I mean. We'll need help if those *pendejos* look like they're going to make a move."

"And you will get it. Matter of fact, tomorrow. It's not all I have in the works, but I think you'll be pleased. I've pulled some strings and Topaz Sawyer arrives on the plane we're flying out on."

"Yes!" Jan and I yelled and gave each other high fives.

"But," I said, "she's a cop. How did you get anyone

to let her come down here?"

"She's gonna be on loan to Homeland Security. Topaz is perfect for the job. She knows the border problems first hand, is cozy with the Border Patrol, speaks Spanish like a native and, quite frankly, isn't an obvious threat."

Yay! Help, in the form of a tiny but mighty female, was flying in to save the day. Kinda like Mighty Mouse.

Chapter Eleven

ROGER AND CRAIG contriving to send Topaz Sawyer to La Paz was a stroke of genius. The woman, a perfect foil for a bunch of *pendejo* bird smugglers who required some serious comeuppance, was also a friend.

Jan and I first met the small in stature, but big on *cojones*, Arizona cop after I'd let loose a barrel full of rock salt and bacon rind into an intruder's nuts. There is little more comforting to me when threatened by man or beast, than the unmistakable sound—PCHK! PCHK!—of a pump action shotgun being chambered prior to some serious badassery. The dude survived, but I was told he walks with a decided limp.

Topaz, a diminutive deputy with an unruly mess of hair closely resembling that of a long-haired German Shepherd, was the investigating officer on scene. I'd called 9-1-1 the minute I knew Jan and I were under threat, so the law arrived at about the same time I dropped the perp.

I'd rented a house in southern Arizona while working at a copper mine on the Mexican side of the border. When she arrived that night, she led me to a dining room chair, asked if I'd like some water, and calmly began asking for details of the incident. What I really wanted was a stiff shot of anything *but* water.

Jan was escorted by a second officer into an office on the other side of the house for questioning. My guess was they separated us to see if our stories of the night's events meshed. I was almost positive they would, for this was one of the rare times we could actually tell the truth, the whole truth, and nothing but the truth. That is, if Jan didn't choose to lie, which was always a possibility. I'd taught her well.

After an hour of telling Deputy Sawyer my side of the story, twice, she asked, "Do you make it a practice to leave your garage door open?"

I told her no way, no how. "In fact I always make certain it is not only closed, but I also lock the door leading from the garage to the main house. I'm a security freak."

She said, "Hmmmm," and called in a third deputy. When he joined us she asked him about the garage door and the door leading into the house. "Garage door was open, but the inner door from the garage into the house was scratched up pretty good. From the looks of it, someone tried and failed to gain entry, and then used a bump lock on the front door instead."

In response to my puzzled look, she clarified, "As in, bump-locked it."

"Bump-locked? What the heck is that?"

While Officer Sawyer jotted a note on her growing

incident report she explained. "A bump-lock master-type key you can buy on the internet that, inserted into the lock and then bumped with a special tool, allows the key to turn. Takes only a few seconds. We've seen a few break-ins we suspected were bumps, but this is the first time we caught the guy with the key."

Her cohort nodded and grinned. "Yeah," another said. "Not only that, he evidently had your garage door opener, but thanks to a better bolting system on the fire door into the house, he couldn't bump the lock. We found the opener next to his SUV. Any idea how he got it?"

"Yes. My Volkswagen was stolen in Mexico and the garage opener was in it."

That was my truth in a nutshell. I wasn't about to volunteer that we were being chased by a couple of bad guys down there, and before it was over, there were cartel members, federales, a jihadist, and a real cranky Texas long horned steer involved. TMI, in my estimation.

Jan was ushered in about that time and heard me. She opened her mouth to comment, but slammed it shut at my warning look.

To steer the conversation elsewhere, I said something like, "This dude who broke into my house must be a stone moron. And a deaf one, to boot. There is an ADT sign outside, stickers on all the windows, and when he opened the front door, that jillion decibel alarm went off. My ears are still ringing."

"He probably wasn't expecting you to be armed."

Jan grinned. "Hetta's always armed. It's one of the

reasons I hang out with her."

I shrugged. "Hey, my daddy always said some folks'll think you're paranoid if you carry a gun, but if you have a gun, what the hell do you need to be paranoid about?"

Topaz asked if there were other firearms in the house.

"Only a .38 revolver, which is in the office, a 30-30 in the hall closet, a .22 automatic in my bedroom, and a pellet pistol in the garage, for pigeons. I hate pigeons. Oh, and, uh, a 9mm Springfield XDM."

Deputy Sawyer perked up. "An XDM? I wish I had one." Her smile then widened. "So why rock salt and bacon rind in the shotgun?"

"My grandmother says that's the way to load, you know, just in case. First you hit 'em low with the salt and rind, then if they don't go down, let 'em eat buckshot."

"You must have some family," Topaz said, but again, there was a note of humor. "I'd say the intruder was lucky to make it out of the house. *If* you can call stumbling right into the loving arms of a border patrol agent lucky. You called the Border Patrol after you dialed 9-1-1?"

"A gal cannot have too many armed good guys about. I figured the BP might respond first since they are all over the area."

"Miss Coffey, do you have any idea who this person might be?"

I shook my head. "It was dark. You think he was just some druggie, and not someone targeting us?"

Sawyer shrugged. "We don't know yet. Do you have any reason to believe it was personal?"

I shook my head, but Jan mumbled, "Is there a cow in Texas?"

"Excuse me?" Topaz asked.

My under-the-eyebrow squint shut Jan up.

She wandered into the office and ordered a bump-lock key off the internet.

We always make the best of learning moments.

Anyhow, that little incident sealed a friendship with Topaz that was to pay off in spades down the line. She'd even come to Mexico once before to help us out of another jam. Okay, so I didn't exactly tell her it was a jam; I just invited her to join me and Jan for several fun-filled days in sunny Baja.

She's evidently since forgiven us for getting her tied up and held captive.

Oh, and for introducing her to the shady, but handsome in a criminal kind of way, Nacho. Evidently whatever happened between them did not end well. Jan and I were just dying to know why.

Chapter Twelve

BECAUSE THEIR PATHS were briefly crossing, we held a meeting at the La Paz airport when Topaz deplaned before Craig and Roger boarded for Bisbee via Tijuana.

After we brought Topaz up to date on the latest intel we had from Rancho Los Pajaros, we waved the guys bye-bye and drove to the boat for a couple of welcoming drinks before taking Topaz to the condo.

"*Salud*, Chica," I toasted after handing her one of our cocolocos.

"Thanks, I'm glad to be here. I think. Last time my so-called vacation didn't go all that well."

"I've been meaning to ask," Jan said. "Just what happened between you and Nacho? You two took off together and the next thing we know, you seemed to be kaput."

Topaz sipped her drink. "Sorry. If I tell you, he'll have to kill you."

"Funny," I said, "that's exactly what Nacho said."

"Good. Now I don't have to kill *him*. And for your edification, we are just friends. Now, let's get down to business. I got the basics on this bird thing, but we need more information before we call in the *federales*."

"Whoa! *Federales*? That seems like *such* a bad idea!" I was thinking that bringing my precious self to the attention of a bunch of cops who already seem to think Mexico would be better off without me could never turn out well.

Topaz read me like a book. "Relax, Hetta. We'll all be out of the picture by that time. We're just the snoop patrol."

"Hetta's really good at that," Jan said.

I started to protest, but she was right. "Uh, does that '*we*'" in '*we'll all*' be out of the picture happen to include Jan and me?"

She cocked her head like the German Shepherd her hairdo was reminiscent of. "Well, us. You, me, Jan, Craig and Roger. I don't…oh! You were thinking maybe I might get Nacho involved?" She blushed. *Hmmm.*

Jan and I, never ones to let a blush go unquestioned, pounced like the media on fake news.

We walked Topaz over to Rhonda's condo and helped her get settled in.

Roger and Craig left wine, beer, and snacks in the fridge, and had changed the sheets for her. We bid her good night, made arrangements to meet for breakfast at the Dock Café the next morning, and returned to *Raymond Johnson.*

As soon as we exited the condo building to take Po Thang for his last walk of the night, I asked, "Do you honestly believe she spent an entire week with Nacho and there was no hanky panky?"

"Might I remind you, Miss Hetta, we've spent several weeks with him without any hootchie-cootchie."

"Yabbut, we are not exactly single. I say either one of them is gay, or she's a better liar than we are."

"Come on, no one is better than we—"

Po Thang cut in front of Jan, almost tripping her and dislocating my shoulder in his haste to rudely sniff a poodle being walked by a fashionable young Mexican couple. The woman scooped up her little frou-frou and gave my dog a dirty look. He whined. Unrequited love's a bitch. No use telling those folks that Po Thang is just overly friendly.

Back on the boat, I massaged my shoulder and groused, "I hate to admit it, but we're either gonna have to get this dawg a shock collar or quit feeding him. What do ya think he weighs now?"

"Too much. Craig mentioned that Po Thang needs more exercise." She gave me a once over and added, "Wouldn't hurt you, either. All that huffing and puffing up that hill when we were checking out the bird sanctuary."

"Oh, give it a rest. Po Thang and I'll both slim down when we get away from the dock, and especially the Dock Café. I plan our departure the minute we deal with those bird rustlers. And just who, besides your anorexic self, says I'm too fat?"

Trouble burst into a raspy rendition of the old-time polka, "I Don't Want Her, You Can Have Her, She's Too

Fat For Me." Jan roared and clapped approval. I gave Trouble his good night treat despite the insult, shoved him in his cage, and threw a blanket over it to shut him up.

Po Thang whined for his before-bed treat. I gave it to him and huffed, "And speaking of bad guys, this *mañana* stuff is wearing on my last nerve. For all we know, those rat bastards could be drugging and loading up the birds as we speak."

"Let's sleep on it. Right now, I'm so tired my brain's scrambled."

"I shall refrain from the obvious blond-slash-scrambled-eggs riposte."

"And I shall refrain from shoving your oversized butt overboard."

Jan, brain-scrambled or not, had made a point.

I did huff and puff up that mountain.

Po Thang was looking a little puffy, as well.

My new jeans, when I finally dared to try them on—I'd been living in winter sweats for the most part since returning from Europe—were *way* too tight.

I woke early, spurred on by the idea of a much-needed lifestyle change.

Po Thang, slightly grumpy at being shaken awake when it was barely dawn, perked up when he realized a walk was in order. I put on my Fitbit and took him for a brisk walk along the *malecón*. That brisk part did not set well with him however, since I sternly refused to let him sniff every telephone pole, bench, and dog along the way.

As soon as we returned to the boat, I steamed broccoli and carrots and mixed them with his dry dog food and a dab of fat-free yogurt. He took one sniff, turned up his nose, and went out on deck where he sat pouting and sniffing the air, sniveling at the scent of sizzling bacon on other boats.

I fed Trouble in his cage, which pissed him off as well, but I knew if he came out and started nibbling on jerky—I bought local stuff in lieu of Oh Boy! Oberto—my dog would somehow end up with it.

Jan dragged herself into the main saloon, rubbing her eyes. "Jeez, Hetta, what the hell time is it? And what is that stink?"

"Just doing what you so rudely suggested last night. Starting a new life style for me and my pooch." I pointed to Po Thang's untouched bowl and showed her my own veggie plate.

She bent down and squinted. "Po Thang threw up in his bowl?"

"Nope, that's his healthy breakfast."

"I thought I smelled bacon."

"Not on this boat. As of today, we're going vegetarian. Well, except for Trouble but, he mostly likes fruit and veggies anyhow. Besides, he doesn't need to lose weight."

"Neither do I." She grabbed her sunglasses and flip-flops, checked her pocket for money, and left the boat.

"Hey, Miz Jan. the Dock Café doesn't open until 6:30. I made coffee."

She stomped back into the galley. "Please don't

tell me it's decaf."

"I do have my standards." I poured her a mug of super dark roasted Mexican coffee, she opened the fridge and took out her half and half. "Oh, thank God. I was afraid you'd thrown it away."

"Nah. But I used powdered milk myself. One percent fat. And Stevia."

"Have you read the label...oh, never mind. I will support you one-hundred percent in your endeavor to get fit, but I think we should hit the grocery store for chicken and fish. At least for Po Thang. He's a carnivore, for cryin' out loud. I will not be a part of this, this," she pointed at my dog's admittedly nasty-looking breakfast, "dawg torture. Call Craig. He'll tell you what to feed a fat dog."

I started to protest Po Thang wasn't fat, just fluffy, but I'd overused that description for myself. "I'll consult with Craig, okay!"

"So," she sipped her coffee and moaned with pleasure, "have you weighed?"

"No, I don't want to start off a diet all depressed."

While Jan went to meet Topaz for breakfast, I threw myself into a cleaning frenzy. I find putting your surroundings in order makes for better mental strength. Jan says there isn't that much Mr. Clean in the world.

While I vacuumed and scrubbed, Po Thang pouted. He somehow knew Jan was off for food, and he wasn't getting any.

By the time she and Topaz returned, I was

exhausted. And starving. I stared longingly at them, as did Po Thang. "Uh, you didn't by any chance bring leftovers, did you?"

"Hetta, it's only nine thirty. You've been on a diet for three whole hours." She looked at Po Thang's still untouched bowl. "And feed that crap to the fish. I'll scramble you both some eggs."

Topaz watched me scrape Po Thang's bowl into the trash. "Good grief. What is that?"

"Never mind. We have to call Craig for some nutritional advice."

Po Thang and I hoovered our eggs—scrambled in a non-stick pan with onions and fresh basil—and I took him for another brisk walk. As we passed the Dock Café, we both whined.

By mid-afternoon, despite some dry dog food for him and two yogurts for me, both our stomachs were grumbling. This was not going to be a fun month. Week. Day? Why didn't I weigh both of us earlier? I mean, if we stick to our diets for one whole day, the start numbers might be skewed.

"Okay, Jan, since you're leaving tomorrow, and Topaz is here for dinner, I've decided to start our diets in the morning. You can help me weigh Po Thang then; you get on the scale and I'll hand him to you. I mean, if we don't have a starting number, how are we going to stay on track?"

Jan sniffed the air. "Do I smell a hint of irrational justification?"

Dinner was broiled fresh snapper, salad, saffron rice, and a mixture of stir-fried, leftover carrots and broccoli. I had to admit the veggies were much better sautéed in olive oil. Po Thang steadfastly abstained from eating until I added a can of dog food to his fish and rice.

Had we not opened that bottle of wine, I would have felt positively saintly. Well, except for that tuna fish sandwich I had mid-afternoon.

With Jan returning to the whale camp to help Chino with the chores, we needed a plan of action. I was tired of waiting around for something to happen with the birds, as were Jan and Topaz.

"How about we go with you as far as Loreto?" Topaz asked Jan. "I can rent a car, take a ride up to the aviary, and pose as some kinda bird nut. At least we'll have an on-site evaluation."

I wasn't for it. "You just gonna saunter into the lion's den? How will we know you won't end up at the bottom of a dry well or something? We need to think this through."

"I'll take Po Thang with me for protection."

Po Thang cocked his head and stood up at the mention of his name, especially when that someone sat at a dinner table. He leaned against Topaz's leg and put his head in her lap.

Jan tipped her own head. "Ya know, an on-site gander isn't such a bad idea, but I think Hetta needs to go to Loreto, as well."

"What am I going to do with Trouble? I already locked him up when we went up there last week. Not fair to do it to him again."

Trouble glided from his perch on high and landed on Topaz's shoulder, walked down her arm, and hopped onto Po Thang's head. We all sucked in our breath.

"Topaz," I whispered, "don't move a muscle, and close your eyes. That bird can be lethal and he might mistake you for an enemy agent."

Topaz froze and squinted. At least she wouldn't lose an eye in the impending dust up.

"Po Thang! Sit!"

And he did.

"Good dog!"

Po Thang looked a little confused, since it was Trouble who gave him the command and praise.

The two former foes, after both enjoying a nosh of jerky, cuddled up on the settee while their humans discussed the dire situation at the bird sanctuary.

Jan called a woman we'd met in Loreto who had a two-bedroom casita for rent near the beach, and she agreed to a dog and bird, as long as we didn't leave them alone in the house. By the time we retired for the evening, we didn't have a plan, and we were sticking to it.

We all agreed that telling Craig and Roger about this little foray was unnecessary because they'd tell us it was a bad idea. But, by golly, we figured a possibly bad idea was better than no idea at all.

Chapter Thirteen

WE LEFT AT oh-dark-thirty for Loreto.

Jan drove her Jeep with Po Thang happily riding shotgun and the rest of us followed in my pickup.

It was still cool out, but Jan was bundled up in the drafty Jeep and Po Thang was as happy as, well, a dog with his ears flapping in the wind. He wore a pair of new bright blue Doggles; Craig insisted if my dawg was going to be riding around with his head out the window, he needed to wear eye protection. When Craig gave them to him, I had serious doubts Po Thang would wear them without a fight, but he seemed to like them. Jan added a natty cravat to complete the look.

At Ciudad Constitución, we picked up four bars from a cell tower, so Topaz, not letting on what we were up to, checked in with Roger for updates from Drew. We couldn't, without internet, pick up his daily report. According to the mule skinner, there had been no further movement of vehicles, and the birds were being well cared for. None, as far as he could tell, had died from their ordeal.

"At least that," I said after Topaz gave me the latest. "Maybe we're a little premature with this trek."

Topaz disagreed. "I want to get a look for myself. I'm operating on second hand info."

"Yep, and I'll just feel better knowing they're safe for myself. I really, really, hate sitting around doing squat. Makes me feel helpless and when I do, Jan says I'm dangerous. I'll admit it, I'm ready to storm the gates, kick those bastard's asses, and get the poor birds back where they belong."

"Won't get any argument here. But getting them returned to where they came from? That might be a tall order. How do we know they were wild caught, and not stolen pets?"

I hadn't considered that. "Okay, reboot. Storm, kick, and at least leave them in the safety of the sanctuary. Under new management."

Topaz chuckled. "I've been in law enforcement long enough to know we don't want to get too hasty. Let's just surveille, as planned, and then decide how and when to kick some butt, okay?"

"I guess you're right. After all, you're the professional," I said, but grudgingly.

"Hetta, why do I get the feeling you're just trying to placate me?"

"Because I am placating you." I gave her a grin. "But we'll do it your way. For now."

"Good."

"So, how *do* you want to handle this?"

"Like we agreed, I'll drive to the Rancho and you

watch me from your lair. Jan can wait at the rental house with Trouble. That way, should we need the marines, she can call them in."

"Mexican, or American?"

"Who cares, as long as they are on our side."

Except, like most well-laid plans, ours went to hell in a tortilla basket.

We were tailing Jan's jeep when she suddenly swerved off the road. We skidded to a stop behind her, and she gave us some bad news. Chino, her sig-other whale guy, had somehow gotten a huge treble fish hook imbedded in his foot. He'd removed it but was on the way to a hospital in Guerro Negro. She was needed at the fish camp, immediately.

"Sorry, guys, but it's the height of the whale count and I have to fill in for him. He can't go out with his crew for several days, because the hospital will keep him around to make sure he doesn't get vibrio vulnificus."

"That sounds like a venereal disease. What's he been *doing* with those whales?"

Jan laughed in spite of her worry. "I'll have to tell him that one, cuz he's gonna need a chuckle. Vibrio is a flesh-eating bacterium that lives in salt water and can infect humans through any cuts or abrasions in the skin. I doubt we have to worry, as the Pacific is cold this time of year, but we have to be very careful. Damned hook got him in a bone and people have died from complications of just that thing."

"Oowie. That had to smart. Okay, hit the road,

Chica. Po Thang come on. Get in the back seat with Trouble and don't start any crap, you hear?"

Po Thang bounded from the Jeep and into my tiny jump seat, most of which was full of Trouble's cage. Trouble grumbled as my dog wedged himself in. I transferred our luggage, supplies, and the like into my camper shell from the back of the Jeep, we hugged Jan goodbye, and off she went, back to her honey.

As we watched her leave I asked, "So, what's plan B, Miss Topaz?"

"We settle in to our rental digs, drink a beer, eat, regroup."

"I like it, except for the order. I vote we drink beer, eat, settle, then regroup."

"Approved."

After stuffing ourselves with carnitas we'd picked up in Loreto, we relaxed on the third-floor, sea view patio.

Trouble was caged inside because there was a light breeze, and I was also afraid he'd take a flying poop over the upscale furniture or chew up something wooden. On the boat, I cover everything with tarps when he's loose, and I keep tabs on him in case he decides to use my teak for a chewy toy. Now we were in strange territory with a hefty security deposit at stake, so he'd just have to get over being incarcerated for *my* own good.

The jailbird grumbled occasionally to let me know he wasn't pleased, but it was somewhat half-hearted, what with his cage chock full of jerky.

"Okay, Topaz, since no one but Jan knows what

we're up to, why don't you give me the coordinates of that road we think we found on Google Earth, and I'll send them to her."

She moved her cursor and clicked on a two-tire track off the main dirt road leading to Rancho Los Pajaros, and before the entrance to Campo Muleshoe. She read off the numbers and I punched them into both our phones.

"What did you label the turn?" she asked.

"Bad Road exit off Main Bad Road. Now, I need a waypoint for where we think we can see Rancho Los Pajaros from on high."

That done, she got out a pad and pen and drew a rough map. "So, we both drive to this spot, then climb up here. I think I see a faint animal path." She drew a circle. "When we're sure we have a good visual on the bird sanctuary, I'll drive there in the rental car and try to worm my way in. Or at least get a glimpse inside the property."

"That's the part I'm worried about. Those guys are thugs."

She gave me a look. "Hetta, I'm a cop. I thrive on thugs."

"If you say so. Anyhow, once I see you leave Rancho Los Pajaros, I'll drive to the main road and we'll rendezvous there for the trip back to Loreto."

"That's the plan, Stan."

"It's going to be a long day. While you're renting a car, I'll hit the grocery store for extra water and victuals.'

"We aren't going on safari here."

"Yabbut I like to be prepared. Besides, I don't think you want me seen by the rental personnel. I sorta have a history with them. I got one of their cars blown up."

She laughed. "I can see how that might be a problem. Okay, you shop, I'll get a car."

"What time should we be there?"

"Eight."

"Then we'd better hit the sack soon. I'll have to leave my phone on for a while, cuz Jan's supposed to call me when she gets to the whale camp. I figure a couple more hours. Right now, I gotta walk the hound."

We were staying two blocks from the Loreto *malecón*, or waterfront, so Po Thang and I headed for the water. I called Jenks as we strolled, not letting on where we were, or what we planned to do. I just wanted to hear his calming voice before I engaged in something that might end badly. I did tell him Jan left for the whale camp because Chino managed to lodge a treble hook in his foot.

"Ouch!"

"Ya think? And, he's out of action for a few days so she has to fill in. High whale season, you know."

"What are you up to? Must be a little dull with Jan gone and Po Thang and Trouble in a ceasefire."

Oh, hell. Should I, or shouldn't I? If I don't tell him and he finds out, he'll know something's afoot, but if I do he might think something's af—

"Hetta, you still there?"

"Topaz Sawyer is here," I blurted.

"That cop from Bisbee? She on vacation?"

"Uh, yes."

"Well, that's good. I know you get a little lonely at times."

"Times when you aren't here." *Crap, that sounded petulant.*

"Speaking of, I think I'll get to La Paz in a couple of weeks. How's that?"

"That. Is. Fabulous. Po Thang! Leave that poodle alone!"

"Mind your pooch, Red. I gotta go to a meeting anyway. I'll talk to you in the morning. Love you. Bye."

I said, "Bye" to one of those foreign phone beeps and dragged Po Thang toward our digs for the night, telling him, "Forget it, Romeo. If I can't get any lovin', neither can you."

Chapter Fourteen

BY TEN THE next morning, we'd picked up the rental, stashed all the food, water, and beer I bought, and caravanned as far as Mission San Javier. After a potty break, we grabbed some breakfast at the little café there, and walked Po Thang again. He must have missed a flower pot the first time.

"Hetta, you lead the way from here. Once we take the turnoff onto the badder road from the sort of bad road, I'll mark waypoints as we go. I suggest you do the same, just in case."

"Just in case of what?"

"I dunno. Just seems like a good idea. We might have to do this again at night or something."

I loaded Po Thang into her car. I figured why put up with two critters when I could fob one off. Moving Trouble's cage into my front seat so he could keep me company, I took off with Topaz following at a dust-free distance.

As we approached the turn off, Topaz called on the VHF radio. "You see it yet?"

"No, I—wait, there it is. I'll stop so we know if your waypoints need tweaking."

Our inputted coordinates were amazingly close; in fact they were correct within a few feet. Google Earth rocks!

Unfortunately, the "road" *was* rocks. No more than a washed-out goat path. After an hour we could go no further in our vehicles and were still a good quarter mile from where we thought we'd have to climb to high ground.

When we got out for a much-needed stretch, I told her, "I was afraid of this. Topographically, I thought it looked a little on the steep side, but between the boulders and angle, it would take an off-road vehicle to go any further on wheels.

"The good news is, it isn't far to the top. Let's take a look."

"I guess Trouble will be okay if we leave the windows down. It's nice and cool up here." I pointed to a scrubby tree. "I'll park under that. Come on, Po Thang, you get to go with us."

"Aren't you worried about him taking off after critters?"

I clipped on his leash. "Not now."

The climb looked much easier than the one we took the last time we spied on the bird sanctuary. And we didn't have to ride mules. I'd have to give Roger some crap about that.

I checked my phone for service. We had three bars. Bless Carlos Slim's greedy little heart; he'd installed cell towers all over the place in order to capture even more pesos. Every cowboy and mule skinner in the Baja now had a cellphone and paid exorbitant rates for the privilege.

Topaz brought up the coordinates we'd put in the night before and made a beeline up the hill, Po Thang on her heels. I let him pull me up the path. Once in a while he gave me a dirty look over his shoulder. I gave him one back. "What? You've never heard of service dogs?" Besides, to get all the equipment we needed up there, we'd have to make two trips, so I was pacing myself. On the next climb, he'd have his saddlebags packed with his treats, water, and whatever would fit.

We set up shop on a ridge. We were further away from the sanctuary than we'd been last time, but with the assist of Roger's super-duper binoculars, we had a pretty good view. There were no humans in sight at the ranch, and no yellow "taco" truck like we'd seen on the last trip. I did make out brightly colored birds flitting around in the aviary, but with the breeze at our backs, we couldn't hear them.

"So, the scene of the crime," Topaz said dryly after taking in what resembled a pleasantly bucolic painting of a lazy Mexican rancho. She handed me the binoculars.

"Sure looks more peaceful than the last time we saw it."

"Is there even the *slightest* possibility that those men were good guys dropping off a load of birds rescued *from* smugglers?"

"I'd almost buy that theory, except for Humberto

and Anna, and his coded message."

"How *exactly* did that go?"

She was starting to annoy me, which is what happens when someone questions the veracity of (in my not so humble opinion) my superior cognitive content. "What do you mean?" I asked, trying and failing not to sound testy.

Topaz picked up on my irritation and shrugged. "Just the cop in me. Can you recall the exact words of the conversation? Just double-checking nothing was lost in translation, Chica."

I relaxed and closed my eyes, recalling that day. "Okay. The phone rang, and since my caller ID said *Rancho Los Pajaros*, I quickly answered and hit the speaker button so Jan could hear what was coming down. I said, '*¡Hola!*' but didn't get a chance to greet Humberto, because a rough-sounding dude interrupted me and rattled something off in rapid Spanish.

"Jan's Spanish is way better than mine, especially with mainland dialects. She mouthed that I should ask who was talking."

Topaz nodded, seemingly approving of our methods. "Go ahead."

"So I asked the caller, *'¿Quien habla?'* but all I got was silence. I thought maybe they'd hung up, then we heard whispering in the background, and scuffling noises. Then Humberto asked, "*¿Señorita Café?*"

"How did you know it was Humberto?"

"For one thing, he steadfastly refuses to address me as *Señora,* like every other Mexican man I know, and he was kicked in the throat by a horse when he was a kid, and he sounds like he has oatmeal stuck in his gullet. It also makes him talk very slowly in order to be understood."

"Okay, what next?"

"After he asked if it was me, I asked *him*, in English, if he was okay and he answered, in Spanish, that he didn't speak English. I know for a fact that he has a good command of the English language; he was raised in Texas, for cryin' out loud. So, as we suspected, something was rotten in Mexico."

"Certainly sounds like it." She was watching the ranch through the binocs while I told my story.

"Anyhow, I asked him, again, in English, how my little parrot, Trouble was doing and he told me Trouble was 'fine and happy and playing well with his bird friends.' At that point, Jan gave a 'cut-it-short' sign, so I thanked him, and then told him to give my regards to his wife, Paula. He said he would. Problem is, his wife's name is Anna."

Topaz lowered the binoculars. "No wonder Jan said you two smelled a *zorillo*."

"Yep, skunk all over it. She also said that Trouble takes after me and does not make nice with those of his species."

"I can testify to that," Topaz said, with a grin.

"I have to admit, Trouble doesn't acknowledge he *is* a bird and prefers to spend most of his time at the house with Humberto and Anna."

"I think I'd better get on the road, so let's get the rest

of the gear up here. I'm going to put my phone on vibrate but call every ten minutes until you see me at the gate. You think we'll have a signal?"

"I certainly hope so, but one never knows up here. Trust me, I will be watching and videoing. Before I forget, there are a couple more things I think you should take with you."

"What?"

"Po Thang, and this." Her eyes widened when I handed her my .380 and two extra magazines from my jacket pockets.

"Where in the hell?—never mind. Nacho, of course. Thanks, I was feeling a little naked." She tucked the small gun into one of her boots, and the spare magazines in the other.

"Just be careful. I'll keep the tracker for Po Thang's GPS, and be sure to turn on his critter cam before you get to the gate, okay? I won't be able to watch in real time, but we'll have a download for later, when we get back to our computers. I'll keep Jan clued in as best I can. I still have a solar charger in the car, and enough bars to reach her."

After we got the rest of our gear up the hill and set up the cameras and paraphernalia we might need, I hugged her and handed her Po Thang's leash.

"You two take care of each other, okay? *Via con Dios.*"

As I watched them take off down the hill, I had a moment of abandonment. We'd lugged Trouble's cage up the hill because I was afraid to leave him in the car for long, but he was covered in case he made too much noise.

"Just you and me, Kid. Want a beer?"

"Ack! Oberto!"

Chapter Fifteen

BEFORE TOPAZ LEFT, she'd helped me assemble Roger's fancy-schmancy camera with that serious telephoto lens. He'd left it behind in La Paz with a great deal of trepidation, saying he should probably demand I write a check for twenty grand to cover the cost in case I lost or destroyed it. Why don't people trust me? Never mind.

We adjusted the heavy tripod and eyecup to my height and dogged everything down tight. I zeroed the lens in on the sanctuary, which was well within range, and since I had no idea what I was doing, we locked in. Unlike the experienced Roger, I wouldn't be panning or zooming, even though he tried his best to teach me how. Quite frankly I was cowed by the ridiculously expensive camera, so we'd have to live with the still shots I captured. At least I knew the images would be sharp and clear, even if they were static.

I took a couple of practice shots, rolling my finger on the shutter release like Roger told me, instead of jabbing it like I was squashing a bug. This I could do, because it was like pulling the trigger on a gun with steady pressure instead of jerking it like a novice shooter.

Once I was satisfied with my camera prowess, I took time to make myself as comfortable as one can get while perched on lava rock. I unfolded a camping chair, grabbed a bottle of water, checked on Trouble, and braced the binoculars with my elbows to save stress on my neck and back.

It was so quiet, I heard Topaz's rental car for a long time after she left, and then nothing but wild bird calls and an occasional rustle in the brush I'd rather not think about. The sky was an unbelievable blue, and contrasted against the brown jagged mountains, made for a breathtakingly wondrous vista. The crystalline air and a snow-capped peak way off in the distance were reminders that it was still winter in the Baja.

I was just about to nod off when the breeze clocked around, as it does every morning, and I was shaken from my stupor by parrot squawks and farm sounds from the oddly contrasting verdant valley below. I leapt to my feet—okay, I clumsily pushed myself to standing—and took a look through the telephoto lens.

One of the *Pendejos* carried a couple of large trays, heaped with fruit, across the yard toward the enclosure, as birds loudly demanded he hurry it up. The punk had a large semi-automatic rifle strapped across his back. I snapped a series of shots, hoping to catch his face when he butt-pushed the gate open while holding the trays. So, Drew was right, the birds were being well fed.

But then a bolt of adrenaline surged through me like

a shot of cocaine. Uh, so I've been told.

Where were the tarps Drew told Roger about? And the heaters? The morning had been chilly, and it must have dropped to near freezing during the night. I adjusted the telephoto lens with clammy fingers, but there was still no sign of warming gear. What the hell?

I was so preoccupied with this confusing revelation that it took a minute for me to register the sound of a toiling engine.

A glance at my watch told me it was a good fifteen minutes too early for Topaz's arrival, so I grabbed the more mobile binoculars again and concentrated on the road below. A cloud of dust marked where the sound was coming from and I zeroed in. In just seconds, a medium-sized yellow truck rumbled into sight and repeatedly sounded his "La Cucaracha" horn.

Two goons slouched out of the ranch house, opened the main entry for the "taco" truck, let the driver enter the enclave, and relocked the gate.

I speed dialed Topaz, but she didn't answer. "Dammit all to hell, Carlos Slim! Get your act together," I groused. I redialed, but no luck. Trying the VHF, all I heard was static. I checked the map and realized she was probably blocked, as the road followed a dry riverbed. All I could do was wait, watch, take photos and keep my fingers crossed Topaz received my warning messages before she blundered into an active scene.

The yellow truck slowly turned around and backed toward the enclosure, and my heart missed a beat. Whispering to myself, I mumbled, "Please, oh, please, don't let that damned truck be delivering another load of birds." I was tempted to call Roger immediately, but decided to wait until I could tell him what the situation actually was, instead of what my worst fears conjured up.

Suddenly feeling terribly alone and helpless, I let Trouble out for company, but harnessed him.

I checked my phone again, finding a satisfying four bars, so the problem was on Topaz's end. I knew she'd soon get a signal as well, and willed her to pick up, fast.

The brakes squeaked the taco truck to a stop, and the hoodlums rolled up the back canvas. I had a bird's eye view, you should excuse the pun, of a load of boxes piled high with bananas, mangos, and pineapple.

The two young slugs lounged around while the truck driver, a dark-skinned old man who looked like he'd blow away in a light breeze, unloaded and toted the large boxes into the aviary. I calculated each one had to weigh over fifty pounds, but the elderly man handled them with ease. The only effort the guards made to help was to open the gate and shoo the birds away from the entrance while the driver did all the work.

The minute the old man entered the enclosure, the slackers slammed the gate behind him and he was besieged by birds. The sound level went up considerably, but the man didn't seem to mind. In fact, his toothless smile and the way he gently waved the birds away while he filled the feeding trays, showed an empathy I'd not seen from anyone down there so far.

I relaxed a mite until, out from the dark interior of the truck, stumbled a tiny blindfolded woman in a crotch length skirt, halter top, and five-inch espadrilles. One of the guards grabbed her arm and roughly jerked her to the ground, where she tripped and fell. Her yelp carried up on the freshening breeze.

This day just kept getting worse. I stabbed my phone, heard that maddening, "At the beep, please leave a message," and did what it said.

It was time to call Roger, no matter how furious he was going to be with me. If Topaz called back, I could cut him off and warn her away from Rancho Los Pajaros.

"That you, Hetta?"

"Roger," I whispered. "We have a situation."

I was filling him in on our seemingly ill-fated foray, when two more women clutching each other in fear, emerged. The old man pushed in front of the *Pendejos*, and gently helped them down one at a time.

"Standby, Roger. I gotta get some photos of this. I'll lower the sound and put you on speaker." I gave him a running account of what was happening below. "Three, so far. I have a bad feeling there are more. Yep, there's another one. I'd better run down to the car and go after Topaz."

"No!" Roger ordered. "You stay right where you are and take photos. Hang up for now, just in case Topaz calls. I'll try to get you two some help. Stay put now, you hear me?"

"Yes, I hear you."

"Let me ask that a different way. Are you going to do what I say?"

Heaven deliver me from semanticists. "Yes, Roger,"

I sighed, "I'll do what you say. Gotta go, two more women just left the truck."

"I'll call you back. Be sure your phone is on vibrate. Stay safe! Bye."

I plugged my phone into my solar charger and went back to the camera. The girls' hands weren't tied and, evidently, they were told they could take off the blindfolds once they were locked inside the enclosure. All ten of them pulled rags from their eyes at the same time and blinked in the strong morning light. I photographed each one as best I could through the wire cage and swarm of agitated, soaring birds.

While I was snapping away, I heard a sound I never expected to: giggling.

The birds were landing on the women and they were laughing in delight. It was such a strange turn of events that it took me a moment to realize they weren't women at all.

They were little girls.

If my heart kept getting these surges, I was afraid I'd have a stroke.

I grabbed a cold beer to calm my nerves, quickly downloaded the photos to my phone, and sent them to Roger, Jan, Topaz, and myself. I waited for a buzz telling me I had received the pics, but no luck. However, one way or another, *someone* was going to witness this horrible situation. I knew it for what it was: human smuggling of children. Even worse, white slavery. God only knew what fate awaited these kids if we didn't do something. Roger said to sit tight, and I reluctantly agreed he was right, and overruled my driving down the mountain and storming the gate.

Just as the beer was doing its job, Topaz drove into view.

Shaking with emotion, I started clicking the camera trigger. I wanted to scream at Topaz, warn her away, but she was apparently oblivious. She pulled up to the front gate, stopped, let Po Thang out on his leash, and nonchalantly walked him around for a pee or three. I held my breath, hoping against hope she'd notice that truck and leave.

It seemed to me that, for just a few hopeful moments, she was contemplating doing just that, but she'd caught the attention of one of the armed men, who wandered over to the gate. I could tell they were talking and watched as she actually flirted. Po thang seriously wanted a piece of this dude—I could hear him all the way up the mountain—and got shoved into the car for his heroic threats.

Turn on the critter cam! Turn on the critter cam! I chanted under my breath, hoping my mantra floated down into the valley, and into Topaz's brain. *If* it could work his way through all that shaggy hair of hers, that is.

I was in mid-mantra when the low life opened the gate and waved her through.

Oh, hell! Dammit! Crap! And a few other expletives certainly destined to screw with my karmic reincarnation hopes of coming back as my own dog, escaped my lips.

Trouble mimicked me.

However, since I'm not a Buddhist, and the new PC makes it uncool to usurp someone else's *anything*, I was already treading on thin juju.

There I go again.

Dropping the binoculars into my camp chair, I glued my eye to the telephoto lens and watched, with great trepidation, for what came next.

I called Roger back to give him a running account, but since I had basically disabled the panning ability on the heavy camera, and did not dare tinker with it, my view was limited to a straight shot from the front gate to the bird enclosure, with just a corner of the house's front porch in the frame.

They gave a hand motion for Topaz to stay in the car, walked back toward the ranch house, and disappeared from view. While he was gone, Topaz seemed to be fiddling with what I hoped like hell was Po Thang's harness, and critter cam.

She waited in the car as she was told, but I was certain she had the doors locked and the engine running.

At least I hoped so.

Chapter Sixteen

THE MINUTE GOON number one told Topaz to wait where she was and walked out of earshot from her car, I called her on the VHF radio. I knew for sure that, unlike cell service, I was in a direct line of sight to her.

After some static and dead air, I heard, "Hetta, I'm in."

"Topaz, thank God! You have to get out of there. Now! They have captive women in the aviary. This thing has just gotten really dangerous."

"I know. I was watching as they unloaded the women. Just keep an eye on me. Gotta go, here they come."

Much to my dismay, I watched as Topaz stayed put. Po Thang, on the other hand, began bouncing off the headliner and doors when he saw goons one, two, and three coming back. The car windows fogged with furious dog breath and dripped with drool.

The men surrounded Topaz's car, guns aimed at her. Even I could tell these guys were not properly trained from the way they handled their weapons and wondered if they even had ammo. Topaz, however, was a trained professional, I kept telling myself. She can handle them.

Before rolling down her window, she wrapped Po Thang's leash around the passenger seat to shorten his access. Pasting on a smile, and talking to Goon One, she seemed to be apologizing for my badly behaved dog—I just gotta learn to read lips!—right before the thug tried to open the door, found it locked, and reached inside to unlock it. Bad move, dummy!

Topaz must have grabbed his hand, for the window slid closed, trapping him as the car, tires smoking, suddenly sped backward, dragging him along. He screamed and cussed as she hauled him through a cactus garden and crashed through the flimsy gates. I could hear his howling clearly. Oh, wait, that was Po Thang, who probably wanted a piece of that tasty arm.

The other two slackers, most likely reluctant to shoot at a car their friend was attached to, froze in place for a moment, then gave chase, but none too enthusiastically. Movement in the yard caught my eye, and a fourth man ran from the house, took aim, and coolly shot out the rental car's front tires.

The car skidded into a dirt embankment on the other side of the road and came to a stop, covered in pieces of gate, dust, and with Goon One still attached. The man who shot out the tires—I figured he was the boss, so I named him Jefe—shouted orders to his other two minions, but they remained fixed in place.

Topaz slammed the door open, smooshing Goon Numero Uno against the car, and he dropped his gun.

She jumped out, swooped it up and aimed it at the trapped guy's crotch.

Po Thang, now free himself, bounded out of the car behind Topaz and began chomping on the guy's jeans. He might have caught a little flesh by pure accident, because the idiot screamed like the heroine in a chainsaw movie and kicked at my dog with his other foot.

Jefe shook his head in disgust, raised his rifle again and nonchalantly shot the trapped hoodlum in the leg. I'm quite sure OSHA would take a dim view of his personnel skills.

The gunshot shocked my dog into letting go of his prey, and he sprang back inside the car. His frenetic barks upset Trouble, who started jumping up and down on my shoulder and went into that deafening, "Ack! Ack! Ack!" mode he does when frightened.

I grabbed him and turned to put him in his cage to quiet him down, when he escaped my grasp and went airborne, first straight up, then kamikazed directly downward toward Rancho Los Pajaros.

Within what seemed seconds, he was perched in Topaz's thick thatch of hair. This could go very wrong in so many ways; the least of which was Topaz ending up with a bird poop hairdo.

Here's the thing; Trouble detests Mexican men. I mean really, really hates them. Nacho had learned that the hard way the first time they met. Even though Trouble still dislikes him, Nacho has this way of giving Trouble a look that cows even that fierce little creature.

The other two goons, spurred into action by their

boss's threats, finally slowly walked toward the car. The wounded goon sagged into the dirt and passed out, his arm still held on high by the window glass.

Topaz reached inside the car, looked to be turning off the ignition, and raised the Goon's gun over her head in surrender. What the hell?

Trying to keep track of it all, I'd lost sight of Po Thang until I saw that Jefe had rushed the car, snagged Po Thang's leash and looped it over a low tree branch. Po Thang's back feet barely touched the ground. He was thrashing and howling, but when Topaz threw down the gun, Jefe gave the leash some slack, and wrapped it to the tree. All the fight had gone out of my dog, and he slumped onto the ground, panting hard.

After inflicting some minimal head damage to the other two slackers, who ran for the ranch house with the bird from hell on their tails, Trouble gave up the chase and perched in the tree above Po Thang. They exchanged a whine and an "Ack!" and he flew away before anyone could regroup and take a shot at him. I wasn't all that worried because it was obvious none of the bad guys had bird shot, and Trouble had speed and agility on his side.

I'd photographed the entire episode as best I could, but in my excitement, I held down the shutter button so long I heard a warning beep and saw a low battery readout. Removing my phone from the solar charger, I plugged in the camera, but it didn't seem to make any difference. I had some juice left and decided to use it frugally. At least the shots I already had pretty much told the story, so I trained the binoculars on Topaz. Nothing much seemed to be happening. She looked to be talking to the boss man, but he still held the gun on her.

Taking a few deep breaths to settle down, I realized I was shaking. Thanks to that hefty tripod, I was pretty sure my photos were good, in spite of my tremors.

Movement caught my eye as two of the other guys, now free of that pesky bird, rushed Topaz—probably swiftly following orders this time after watching the consequences of displeasing el Jefe—and manhandled her straight into the bird enclosure, locking it behind her.

The aviary was in chaos. The gun shot had terrified both the birds and the girls, so there was a cacophony of shrieks, both human and bird, as the girls covered their heads and batted away parrots of all sorts. Alfred Hitchcock could not have directed it better.

I watched as Topaz brushed herself off and rounded up the girls. She grabbed a tarp, got them in a huddle, and drew it over them. It seemed to calm the youngsters until el Jefe pushed Po Thang in with them and he bounded to join them under the tarp.

Several girls decided to take their chances with the birds; many Mexican children are terrified of dogs. Topaz talked them back to safety, and soon a few of them were cuddled up to my dog. He was amazingly docile after almost being hanged. Hanging will do that to you.

I sat back, grabbed a water, and chugged it. Now what?

And just when I thought things couldn't get worse, I was attacked.

Something hit me in the head and I swatted wildly

before realizing it was a very agitated Trouble coming in for a landing. He quickly worked his way down my shoulder and tucked himself inside my collar. He was wet from stress and panting so hard I feared he'd have a heart attack. I cuddled him, cooing and stroking his neck feathers with water from my bottle. After a few minutes, he drank a little from my hand, and fell asleep.

I put on a jacket and zipped him in, because that earlier light breeze from below had picked up, and the last thing Trouble or any other parrot needs is a drafty chill when they're damp. Poor Trouble was really having a crappy couple of weeks, and mine weren't much better.

Things settled down at the ranch, what with everyone safely tucked away from each other; the *Pendejos* were all in the house, and the women and my dog were sheltered in the bird enclosure. I took one more look and saw the old truck driver, who had been conspicuously absent during the entire brouhaha, standing watch from his covered truck's bed.

It was time to beat feet down the mountain before it got dark.

I sent all the latest pictures out before going back down the mountain. Without anyone to help me carry the heavy equipment and Trouble's cage, I had two choices; make two trips or leave most of it where it was.

Needless to say, I chose to leave the camera, making me thankful I hadn't written Roger that twenty-thousand dollar check he wanted as a deposit. It would have bounced anyway.

Dragging the camera under a creosote bush took a good twenty minutes and zapped my energy. I sat down to rest, then gingerly started my descent on the unstable lava rock trail. I threw the cage in front of me as far as I could, then continued to do so all the way down. I ended up side slipping for at least thirty minutes. Jeez, it only took Topaz ten.

By the time I got to my pickup, my ankles and thighs burned. I put the somewhat worse for the wear cage into the back jump seat and collapsed behind the wheel long enough to check my cellphone for a signal. It was an exercise in futility.

Making sure all the windows were rolled up, I extracted Trouble from inside my jacket and put him into the safety of his cage again. When I threw a blanket over it, he didn't let out a peep.

I was certain I'd find bird poop somewhere inside my clothes later on.

Oh, for a hot shower and a cold beer!

I took a deep breath and hummed the "Marines' Hymn" as I drove away.

"Trouble, we could sure as hell use some of those dudes to storm the Halls of Montezuma once again.

Trouble mumbled a weak, "Semper Fi."

Chapter Seventeen

THE NEAREST PLACE I knew for sure had phone service was Mission San Javier—okay, sort of sure, since one never really knows—or the mule skinner's house. I drove straight for Campo Muleshoe and was about to make the turn at his hand-carved sign, when I spotted a huge cloud of dust to the west on the main road.

Taking no chances of being seen by anyone, I drove into the desert while cursing myself for buying a shiny red vehicle. At least by now it was coated with dust.

Entering an area strewn with humongous boulders, I picked out one with a view of the road and Drew's turnoff and parked behind it. As always, when I saw these boulder fields I wondered what the scene must have been like when they were spewed from a volcano like popcorn; the one I picked was the size of a house. Once safely tucked away, I cut the engine, rolled down the window, and listened.

Whatever was coming my way, it was doing so excruciatingly slowly and noisily. Screeches and growls sent birds airborne and small critters scurrying through the dry brush.

Reaching for a warm sweater from the back seat, I extracted Trouble from his cage and swaddled him in it. He barely moved as I gently placed him in the glove compartment for safety, and to muffle him in case he got the urge to squawk. In truth, it is one of his favorite places in the car, so I'd long ago affixed a latch to the lid so it would remain partially open for airflow while remaining somewhat soundproofed.

Exiting my pickup as silently as possible so as not to disturb my sleeping bird, I snaked my head around the boulder. The large cloud of dust was closer, but I still couldn't see what sounded like a slow-moving vehicle. From the low-grinding engine sound and the oversized dust trail, I was thinking someone might be grading the road. At this hour?

I pulled up my hoodie—red hair, red car, bad combo for stealth maneuvers—and continued my neck-stretch surveillance mode and was about to take a break when a yellow truck crept into view. In valley shade, visibility becomes more difficult as the sun sets, but failing light or not, I was convinced it was the same delivery truck I'd seen at Rancho Los Pajaros.

Watching the familiar taco truck from my hidey hole, I found myself literally caught between a *real* rock and the hard place.

Did I race for an internet or cell connection before the driver saw me bolt, or did I wait for him to pass and tail him, just in case Topaz, Po Thang, and those girls were being relocated to some fresh hell?

Back inside my pickup, I prepared to give chase. Well, *chase* was probably not the operative word, since the truck was doing a whole five miles per hour.

Trouble let out a weak peep when I shut my door. "Go back to sleep my brave little warrior. Looks like it's gonna be a *very* long night."

Listening intently for the truck to finally pass, I heard his brakes shriek to a metal-on-metal halt. Fearing he had somehow spotted me, I started my engine and made ready to rabbit, knowing he'd never catch me in that leviathan he was driving. He'd stopped completely, and fearing he was headed my way on foot, I almost bolted when I realized he was rolling again, and I had to know where.

Leaving the engine running, I exited and dared a peek.

He was turning into the mule skinner's road.

And he was dragging Topaz's car.

Back inside my vehicle, I had a decision to make. Did I stick around and try to see who's in that truck, or drive like a bat outa hell until I got enough bars on my phone to call Roger?

I knew what made the most sense but was hesitant to go that route. My senseless self (the normal one) voted to follow the truck, spy on them, then descend upon them like the Cavalry hell-bent on wiping them from the face of the earth. Until I remembered two things: 1. Topaz had my gun, and 2. Custer.

Tightening my seatbelt and making sure Trouble was

secure, I sneaked out from behind my boulder. Why I sneaked, I have no idea, since the gear-grinding and screech of what I decided were the wheel rims of that rental car over rocks surely overcame any noise my pickup made.

A quarter of a mile later, I stomped on the gas. Driving *way* faster than prudent without headlights on a dark and bumpy road, I also listened for a ping that said I had cell service. I thought for sure I'd get at least a weak signal at Mission San Javier, but no luck.

At the mission I picked up a paved road, so I sped up even more and was straightening out the curves when I topped a hill and got that long awaited ping. Leaving a long length of rubber on the road, I backed up, found a place to pull off and made a call.

"Roger! Thank heavens I reached you. Did you get the photos?"

"Yep, and I've been trying to call ya. Have you lost yer common sense?"

"Jan says I don't have any. I just now got a signal since I left the lookout, and in case I lose you, listen carefully. Do *not*, under any circumstances, call Drew! He's dirty!"

"Well, no kidding. You got the picture to prove it."

"What? One of those guys was Drew? I couldn't make out any faces. They all wore hats and sunglasses."

"Me neither at first, but then I enhanced the photos and low and behold, the guy in the blue shirt was none other than that polecat mule skinner."

"*Pendejo!*"

"You got that right. Truth is, I already smelled a *zorillo*. He'd called me about ten minutes before I got your first batch of pictures and he told me there was no change in the situation. So, a'course, when I got yer evidence to the contrary, I smelled mule poop. I ran a quick background check on him. Skunk's got a rap sheet long as yer arm, mostly for smugglin' of some kind."

"That bastard! We walked right into his hands. Wait, you didn't tell him Topaz and I were making another reconnaissance mission today, did you?"

"How could I? You didn't bother to let me know. Which, by the way, we'll have to have a parlay about later."

"But, it's a good thing I was there to see them snatch Topaz, right?"

"Hetta, they couldn't a snatched her if you two hadn't been wanderin' off the reservation."

He had a point. "Scold me later. So, there is an excellent chance these guys have no idea who Topaz is, right?"

"Not unless she was dumb enough to carry ID."

I glanced at her handbag in the backseat. "Nope, she left everything, including the rental car papers, with me. But she did take my gun."

"Your *gun*? You have a gun in Mexico? Are you nuts?"

"Of course I am. However, the gun is legal, honest."

Loud sigh. "I don't even want to know."

"You betta off, Rog. And, they didn't search her before tossing her and Po Thang into the birdcage. I was watching their every move."

"I'll do my best to get to you by tomorrow. Meanwhile, go back home."

"No way. I'm not leaving the area until I get my dog back. Oh, and Topaz. We rented a house in Loreto and that's where I'm heading right now."

"Why am I suspicious that you gave in too easy? Are you planning on doublin' back."

"Actually, you might want me to."

"What? Why?"

"I had to leave your camera and tripod up on the mountain."

"Whaaaat?"

I ended the call and said to Trouble, who had woken up and was nestled back inside my collar after I'd loosened my seatbelt and let him free, "Well, that went well, doncha think?"

"Ack! Numb nuts."

I am sooo glad my *dog* can't talk."

I had considered, as Roger feared, doubling back to my mountain perch, since I was only about half-way to Loreto. However, an even darker dark had dropped like a curtain. And even though I knew that, when my eyes adjusted, the stars would give me fair light, even then I'd probably break my neck climbing back up that slippery hillside. Or stumble into a rattlesnake den.

Since I found neither of those appealing, and Roger's camera had no infrared capabilities, I reasoned I'd be better able to help Topaz and Po Thang with the morning light.

"Hey Trouble. We're gonna camp out! What an adventure."

"Numb nuts."

Finding a suitable spot just upstream from a small ford, I parked off the road, blew up the self-inflating mattress I keep in the camper shell for just such an emergency, and unrolled a sleeping bag. I grew misty-eyed with gratitude for my dad, who taught me to plan for the worst. And my mom, who insisted I always carry clean underwear.

I locked us inside the camper shell, and shared some of my goodie stash of jerky, Spam, crackers, and bottled water with Trouble. I am a light sleeper, so I figured I'd hear anyone coming down the hill. Hopefully, those a-holes hadn't spirited their hostages away on the road headed west, the one that led to the Pacific coast, but there was nothing I could do about it at the moment. Exhausted, I fell asleep in a flash.

I was awakened at a little after three by the sound of a nearby vehicle. A waxing moon afforded me a good view through the slide-open window into my truck cab; in the Baja the lack of manmade ambient light makes for bright moon shine even during a crescent phase, and I had an almost full moon.

A beat up farm truck lumbered into sight and stopped at the low water crossing. I felt like a peeping Tom as I watched a cowboy-hatted silhouette bend down, scoop water into his hands for a drink, then take a leak in the stream, and drive off. Note to self: never drink downstream from a crossing.

Chapter Eighteen

TROUBLE NIBBLED ON my nose before first light, then crowed like a rooster.

"Egad, Trouble. My eardrums. Okay, okay, I'm up."

I gave him a piece of jerky, ate some myself, wished for a Starbucks, and we hit the road again. I was eager to get a gander at the bird sanctuary, but I slowed down and drove without headlights in the pre-dawn gloom. I was certain I'd see anyone coming my way in plenty of time to hide again. Unless some idiot was driving without lights.

Stiff from a combination of my strenuous day before and sleeping in the camper shell, I knew the climb to my lookout was going to be painful and hazardous. I felt it prudent to leave Trouble in the pickup in case I stumbled and rolled on him. He wasn't happy about it until I threw him the entire bag of jerky.

According to my pickup's thermometer, it was in the low forties, and as I climbed higher it felt even colder. However, my clumsy hiking skills, combined with the rising sun, warmed me in a hurry. In fact, by the time I hit the top and set up the camera, I was perspiring inside my jacket and doubled-up sweats. I removed my jacket and got a whiff of someone in bad need of a shower.

The valley below was still in shadow and there were no lights to define the bird sanctuary. Through the telephoto lens, I made out the outline of the yellow truck and sighed with relief. If the truck was there, it was a good bet that so were Topaz and Po Thang.

Sunrise in the valley gave me a good look at the bird pen and house. Concentrating on the large wire cage, I finally saw Po Thang crawl out from under a tarp, stretch, yawn, and trot over to a water bowl. A couple of minutes later, Topaz stepped into sight. I snapped photos of both of them and the girls as they also emerged and sent them out. My phone had a decent charge from the trip down the hill and back, so I laid down the tripod and camera and left the camera plugged into the solar charger while I slid down to the pickup.

Trouble cussed at me a little for leaving him, but judging by the empty packet of jerky, he hadn't had much time to suffer. Driving back to Loreto was a double-edged emotional sword. I hated leaving Topaz and Po Thang, but it was clear I was helpless to rescue them by myself.

As soon as I got a cell signal, my phone went nuts. I pulled over and read messages from Roger, Jan, and Craig. Jan was almost to the rental house in Loreto, and Roger and Craig would arrive later in the afternoon.

"Trouble, me boy, it looks as though those bad guys are going to get their comeuppance very shortly. What say we celebrate with a great big breakfast after I stop at the feed store and get you a new cage?"

"Trouble is a pretty boy."

"Yes you are. And you've been a very, very, good bird."

He blushed and preened. "Ack! Good Trouble."

I messaged Jan and asked her to meet me for breakfast at Orlando's in Loreto because I love their chilaquiles. I hadn't had a decent meal in for*ever* and felt I rightly deserved fried tortilla chips boiled in heavy cream, then mixed with a zesty red chili sauce and cilantro, and topped with tons of cheese, sour cream, and even more cilantro.

By the time we arrived to meet Jan, she was already there and had ordered me a fruit salad.

There is no justice.

"So," I asked while stabbing a piece of papaya with little more force than necessary, "what's the latest on Chino? How's his foot?"

She raised an eyebrow. "Better than that poor fruit salad you're torturing. Actually, the reason I could return here so fast is because Chino's taken over the laboratory and sent his interns out on the whale count. His foot is healing rapidly, but he can't get it wet yet."

Several platters heaped with something cheesy were deposited on a table nearby. I staunched a rivulet of drool with my napkin and moaned.

Jan snapped her fingers in front of my face. "Hetta, no!"

I threatened her hand with my fork. "I've had a crappily bad twenty-four hours, Chica, and I require real food."

She quickly withdrew those fingers. "Think positive. Maybe you lost a pound or so."

I snagged the waiter on his way by and ordered chilaquiles with extra sour cream.

"*Now* I can think positive."

Back at the rental, we went over the details of my day and night before and studied the photos. While I wasn't able to video, I had the camera trigger, with a push to one side, set to thirty pics a minute so, when laid side by side, they painted a pretty good picture. We'd exhausted an entire color cartridge printing them out.

"I'm glad I brought the printer," Jan said. "Look here, tortilla breath."

"I'll take that as the ultimate compliment," I said. I got my cheaters and bent over the series of pictures she pointed to.

I found myself staring at a long row of shots, the ones of the guy I called El Jefe.

He had a baseball cap pulled low on his forehead, wore sunglasses and held a long gun. I carefully looked at each shot, but it wasn't until one of the last few, when he turned toward the ranch house after shooting his own goon and almost hanging my dog, that I saw it.

"Roger was right. It *is* Drew. I followed those jeans and that belt for hours last week while I was on that fat mule."

"And didn't you think his mule skin belt was a little creepy? I doubt there's another like it in the Baja. And if you remember, I even commented it was kinda weird that a dude living in the middle of freakin' nowhere, running a mule-ride business, would wear Ralph Lauren jeans."

"Bastard!"

"Son of a bitch!"

"*¡Pendejo!* Trouble squawked.

Roger and Craig arrived a little after four, dead tired. They'd driven ten hours to San Diego overnight, then caught the Tijuana to Loreto flight. The house only had two bedrooms, so we let them have one and Jan moved in with me.

Truth was, we were all bushed. We had ideas about what came next but voted for an official nap-time-out. I'd had a rough night in the camper shell, Jan had driven from the Pacific Coast, and the guys only caught an hour here and there. We turned off all phones and devices, and covered Trouble in his shiny new cage.

When I woke at six, everyone, including Trouble, was still snoozing. It was time for a meeting of the minds, so I uncovered and loosed the bird from hell. He headed straight for Jan, woke her with a serenade that sounded like Engelbert Humperdinck with a mouthful of rocks, then, satisfied, he sailed to Roger and Craig's room.

"Hetta!" Roger hollered. "Come get this piece of bird crap before I wring his scrawny neck."

"Never mind," Craig yelled. "We'll be right out, Trouble included."

Jan and I headed for the bar and concocted a huge pitcher of Cocolocos and were having our first one when Roger and Craig arrived.

"Hey, where's the bird?" I wanted to know.

Roger unsnapped his bush jacket's pocket and pulled out a grumbling Trouble. "You mean this one?" He let Trouble go, and he hopped onto my shoulder.

"Oh, poor baby, what did that mean old man do to you?"

"Mean man. Mean man."

Roger walked back into the bedroom, returned with a package of Oberto turkey jerky fresh from the States, and swung it back and forth like a hypnotist's watch.

Trouble's head followed the package as it swayed in Roger's hand, then let gluttony overcome ennui. He flew over and landed on Roger's arm, walked down, and started tearing open the bag.

"Oh, boy, are you easy," I commented.

"Ack! Hetta's easy! Hetta's easy!"

"Okay, Roger, *now* you can wring his neck."

Chapter Nineteen

THE CAMARADERIE OF finally being reunited with Jan, Roger, and Craig gave me an overwhelming sense of relief. I'd had a tough day or two, and while still worried about Po Thang, Topaz, and the whole situation at Rancho Los Pajaros, being with friends gave me comfort. We were laughing over Trouble's antics when my phone rang. I looked at the caller ID and my respite from worry took a powder. I had some 'splainin' to do.

"Hi Jenks," I said. Jan was whisper-singing, "Het-ta's in trouble, Het-ta's in trouble." I sent her a death glare and drew my finger across my neck. Of course, you know who picked up Jan's song, albeit louder and scratchier. Everyone cracked up and Jenks asked, "You having a party?"

"No, it's just Jan, me, Roger, Craig, and Trouble. Roger and Craig like it so much here they came back." Okay, so I didn't say where *here* was, so it was only a tiny little prevarication.

"Great. Where're Topaz and Po Thang?"

"Uh, she took him for a walk." The hem on my

pants threatened to burst into flame. "How'er things in Dubai," I added, quickly redirecting the questioning.

"Same old, same old. But I have some good news. I've been called to a meeting in San Francisco in a few days, so I can come to the boat after. Can't stay long, but sure am looking forward to seeing you, Red. How long are Roger, Craig and Topaz staying?"

"Uh, not sure. But if they're still here when you arrive we'll kick 'em to the beach and take off for the islands. Can't wait to see you."

After we said our goodbyes I faced my jury. They didn't look very forgiving.

Jan raised a perfect eyebrow. "Surely you didn't just tell Jenks that Topaz was out taking Po Thang for a walk?"

"Don't call me Shirley."

"Smarty pants."

"Smarty pants! Ack! Smarty pants!"

I shot both Trouble and Jan the finger and was about to launch into a verbal tongue lashing when Craig stood up, put one hand horizontally over the other, and yelled, "Time out!"

"Time out! Ack! Time ou—" Trouble was cut off as Craig cupped his wings between his huge palms, strode to the cage, and jammed him into it. Striding toward the patio where we all sat with our mouths open, he asked, "Who's next?"

I considered saying something like, "Someone didn't get enough of a nap," but thought better of it; that cage was pretty small. So I said, "You have our undivided attention."

He looked at me like I'd grown another head. "Whoa, this situation has more than *one* of us acting out of character. Look, we're all tired, worried, and feeling helpless. So, let's just get this thing done. Where do we start?"

"*I'm* going to start with an apology for the entire screw-up," I said.

Jan nodded, "Me too."

"Jan, you didn't do anything. It was all me and Topaz."

"Yabbut, if I'd a been here, I wudda."

We high-fived and said, at the same time, "*We* screwed up."

Roger, who wasn't as familiar with our dynamic as Craig had become over the years, shook his head and tried to get the conversation back on track. "Nobody screwed up."

"Huh?" Jan and I said in surprise.

"Let's break it down. If you gals hadn't gone gallivantin' around the countryside, we wouldn't know Drew was dirty. We'd think we were still after bird smugglers and not even know about the human traffickin'. We'd probably be goin' at the whole thing differently, all the while thinkin' we had plenty of time to save the birds. Those girls cudda been long gone. Maybe halfway to the Middle East."

Jan's eyes grew wide. "Middle East? Oh boy, we heard all about that while we were in France. Evidently huge yachts owned by Middle Eastern bigwigs steam into Cannes and other Mediterranean ports loaded with hookers, most of whom are victims of white slavery. And the pimps aboard get a small fortune for their so-called guests to party aboard. We heard they charge as much as forty grand a night."

"So you think the birds are most likely headed to the US, and the girls somewhere else?"

"I'd bet my boots on it."

"And Topaz? What will they do with her?"

"Oh, she's a good lookin' gal, so as long as they don't find out she's a cop, they'll sell her, too. She just won't bring as much cuz she's older."

"Po Thang?"

Craig and Roger exchanged a somber look, and Craig took the lead. "We'll get him back, Hetta."

"And if we don't?" I persisted.

Craig sighed. "Worst case? Dog fights."

I felt faint. "Dog fights? Po Thang hasn't got a mean bone in his body! He wouldn't last…Oh. My. God. They'd use him for bait?"

"No they won't," Roger said quietly, "because we're gonna git him back. Safe and sound."

Jan, who lunged for the drink pitcher the moment our conversation turned to Po Thang's possible destiny, filled both our glasses, and sat close to me on the divan. She patted my hand, lifted her drink, and said, "Safe! And! Sound!"

We all raised our drinks to our new mantra, then got down to devising an attack plan for the next day.

Here's what we came up with: Jan, Trouble, and I'd take

my pickup and return to the overlook where I left the camera the day before, while Craig and Roger rented two more cars. We agreed Jan's Jeep was too distinctive, so they'd leave it parked near the rental agency.

Roger would make a beeline for the mule skinner's corrals, while Craig, in the other non-descript rental, would take a drive by the sanctuary. "Promise us you won't end up in the birdcage with Topaz, Craig," I said, as we all left on our assignments. "And Roger, you're walking into the viper's pit."

"Only the snake don't know that *I* know he's lower than a snake's belly."

"Still, if you guys get shanghaied, you'll have to rely on me and Jan to rescue you."

"Now, there's an incentive to keep our butts free, huh, Roger?"

I lightly slapped Craig's muscular arm with the back of my hand. "Hey! We're…uh, what are we, Jan?"

"Fearless, loyal, and relentless," she boasted.

I chuckled. "I think you just described Po Thang and Trouble."

"Yep. We're the fearsome foursome, primed to save the day."

Craig and Roger exchanged a doubtful glance. "Like Craig said, we'd best stay out of harm's way on our own. Orders of the day, troops! Safe and sound!" He waved his hands like a symphony conductor and we all chanted, "Safe! And! Sound!"

En route from Loreto towards our mountain spy spot,

Troubled sing-songed, ad nauseam, "Safe! And! Sound."

Finally, Jan had enough. She snatched him from his cage and held his beak to her nose. "If you don't shut the hell up, you're not going to be any of those things, ya hear me?"

He gently nibbled her nose. "Ack! Trouble's a pretty bird."

"That's better. For that, you get some of that jerky your uncles brought you." She gave him a piece and plopped him on her shoulder. "And don't drop any on me. Or anything else, for that matter."

"Ack! Trouble's a pretty, pretty, pretty bird." Every pretty went a decibel higher.

I stuck a finger in my ear and said, "I've been thinking."

"That never bodes well."

"Wise ass. We need to devise a plan for the future, which includes Trouble illegally immigrating to Arizona."

"He'll have to get in line."

"Part of Roger's ranch spans the border, and there is only a barbed wire fence. He can fly right on over, and I doubt there's anyone that would take the trouble, you should excuse the intended pun, to shoot him down with a drone."

"So, as a reward and expense for them coming to our aid, we dump the little bugger on Craig and Roger? I like it."

"I knew you would. We've smuggled Trouble across the border before, and we can do it again."

"I might remind you that we all got busted, placed

under house arrest, and Trouble was damned near euthanized by Cochise County authorities."

"We'll be smarter this time."

"Har! Har!" Trouble crowed.

Everyone's a critic.

Chapter Twenty

I'D LEARNED THE hard way the past two days that cell service was iffy in the area where we'd be, so we were all carrying VHF radios with extended antennas, and they were set to marine channel 88—which is seldom used in Mexico—and on low power. The chances of picking up a signal from boats in either the Pacific Ocean or the Sea of Cortez were slim, but we do get bounces, so I chose this rarely used channel, just in case our phones didn't do the job.

After our scramble up that dastardly trail that seemed paved with marbles, Jan and I made camp as livable as possible. She helped me set the camera up and took a quick look at the sanctuary and ranch, while I hooked up all our equipment to solar chargers. This time we brought a laptop computer, as well, and extra batteries.

"What's happening down there?" I asked Jan, as I checked my phone for service and found a less-than-satisfying two bars.

"Real quiet. There's a goon sitting down with his head propped up against the birdcage gate, and he seems asleep."

I was aiming our solar chargers directly into the sun and checking their output into our various devices. "I'm not surprised. Except for Drew, every one of those dudes is five cans short of a six pack. And that idiot asleep with his head up against the gate? Topaz could garrote him in a heartbeat, so she must be waiting for a clean getaway." I heard Po Thang suddenly raising hell. "What's up with the dawg?"

"Oh, hell, he's staring straight up at us. I know he can't see us, but the wind is blowing in his direction, so he's picking up our scent. I'm surprised we can hear him."

"That's his outside, I'm-upset, bark. His loudest."

"Okay, I got an eyeball on Topaz. She's moved next to Po Thang and is hugging him. She obviously knows we're here and is trying to distract him. I cannot believe the guard is sleeping through all the racket."

"Maybe Topaz done did him in?"

"No such luck. Idiot-boy just turned over. Aha, there's an empty tequila bottle by his side. Puzzle solved. Amateur!" Jan snapped off photos and we sent them to Roger and Craig, who were both on their way up the mountain from Loreto in separate vehicles.

I refilled my coffee mug and moved to take over the camera. Just as I did, we heard a new noise below. Po Thang started baying a "someone's coming" warning, but this time he was focused on the main road. Topaz, who had him in a headlock of love, pushed her sunglasses up into that shaggy hair of hers and stared intently in our direction. She gave us a covert thumb's up, which I caught on camera.

"Topaz just telegraphed a sign. She knows we're here, for sure."

"For all the good *that* does," Jan snorted.

"Hey, if I were being held hostage by a gang of lowlifes, I'd garner some comfort knowing friendlies were nearby. I wish we could communicate with her. Oh, oh! She just gave me a 'bang! bang! You're dead!' gesture. She's still got my gun!"

"Now *that's* the best news we've had in days."

"Uh-oh, we got a bandit, Miss Jan!"

"Where?"

"Driving in the ranch entrance gate. That skunk, Drew, just jumped out of his pickup truck. Hoo-boy, he's tearing that guard a new one. Get the binocs. This is too good to miss."

I zeroed in on the dust-up below. Po Thang was beside himself, charging the fence over and over as the derelict guard tried to protect himself from El Jefe by curling into a fetal position. Drew repeatedly kicked him with his silver-encased, pointy-toed cowboy boots. I'd noticed they were very sharp when he led us up the mountain last week, but I didn't think much about them because he never used them on his mule. Finally, Drew ran out of steam and stormed away, leaving the hapless guard in a heap.

Was it only a week ago when we took that ride? Seemed like a year. "I hope Drew shoots the guy like he did the other one. At the rate he's going, there won't be any of his gang of goons left for us to deal with."

"Dang. I was looking forward to that part."

I grinned, knowing full well she meant it. "No honor amongst thieves, and all of that. You wanna switch?

"Sure."

After only twenty minutes with my eyes glued to the camera lens cup, and clicking the occasional photo, I was already in pain. The day before had done a job on my neck and shoulder muscles that no amount of Aleve fixed. I stepped back, rolled my arms, and groaned.

Jan said, "I've got the camera duty. Look in my jacket pocket for a bubble pack of large white pills."

"Got 'em."

"Take one with a lot of water."

"What are they?"

"Truthfully, I have no idea what's in them, but they're over-the-counter in Mexico and work wonders for me and Chino. Take one, Chica. It's gonna be a long day."

"Bless you, Doctor Jan." I popped a Caradoxin and did some more Yoga neck and shoulder exercises. Within a few minutes my neck loosened up and the pain subsided. "Good news, Jan. Those pills do work wonders."

"Oh, oh, Drew is coming back out. Maybe he's not through beating up on that guard."

"Hopefully so."

"Shoot, the guard ran away. Hey, Drew's carrying a large bowl and two cans of what looks like dog food. Even better, he emptied them into the bowl and shoved it into the cage for Po Thang."

"Probably just keeping him fattened up for dog fights," I grumbled. "What else is going on?"

"Drew's chatting with Topaz. Her body language *screams* submissive. Damn, she's good."

"One or both of us should learn to read lips, for sure. Do they have classes for that?"

"Probably. We'll Google it right after we've slain the villains and rescued our damsel in distress."

"Speaking of, any word from the B-team?"

"You okay to take the watch again? I'll check for messages."

I stepped up to the camera just as Drew turned away from Topaz and walked toward the house. Within seconds, Topaz, using hand signals, was communicating with the girls. Smart of her not to admit she spoke fluent Spanish.

"Okey dokey, podner. News from the B team. Roger got our photos, knows Drew isn't at the mule ranch, and is going in to toss the joint. Maybe we'll get a handle on how big this operation is and, more importantly, what they plan to do with everyone in that birdcage."

"Tell him we'll alert him if Drew leaves the sanctuary. And ask him to radio us when he gets to Campo Muleshoe. Just a test blip'll do it, so we know we can communicate."

Jan switched from her phone to her laptop and went to work. After a minute or two, she got a ding. "Aha! Agent Craig has stationed himself out of view on the road between Campo Muleshoe and Rancho Los Pajaros, so if we let him know when Drew leaves, he can do something to slow him down if necessary."

"Like what?"

"Want me to ask him?"

"Nah. Let's just do our part up here. I did enough decision-making yesterday."

"Whaaat? Hetta Coffey, giving up control? Call the networks."

"Oh, shut up. I'm tired, okay?"

"How's about we share camera and binocular shifts, so we have two sets of eyes on the ranch at all times?"

"Good plan, Agent Jan."

"Agent Jan! Ack! Agent Jan!"

"Shut up, Agent Trouble."

Chapter Twenty-one

OUR VHFS CRACKLED with three consecutive bursts of static about ten minutes after we got Roger's last message that he was at the mule skinners place.

"Okay, Agent Hetta, stay sharp. Roger's in. We'd better go into stealth mode. That static sounded awfully loud to me." She turned off her handheld, handed it to me to put on a charger, and moved back to the camera.

I shook off a lethargy that had befallen me while sitting in the warm sun. Plugging in Jan's radio, I inserted my earphones into mine and turned the volume to low, but on high power. "Okay, I'm on radio duty. God, I'd kill for a nap."

"Go ahead. I've got eyes on the sanctuary, my cellphone on vibrate in my pocket, and the radio will wake you up. Grab a quick one while you can."

"Are you sure?"

"Absotively. After this is over, we'll go down to Cabo, check into a luxury hotel and spa, and treat ourselves to a week of nothing. Dream about that."

"Sounds fab, but I'd as soon fantasize about my

upcoming trip to the islands with Jenks. Okay, closing my eyes."

I was just dozing off when a thought hit me like a shockwave. We needed back up! All seven of us (counting Agents Po Thang and Trouble on the roster) were up here in the middle of nowhere, and not one soul who actually might care knew where we were. We could disappear without a trace and only Jenks might have some clue why, but no hard facts. By the time he figured it all led back to Trouble's reappearance, it would be too late.

A sudden image of Po Thang battered and bloodied from a dog fight did the job. I sat up and grabbed the laptop.

"Can't sleep?" Jan asked.

"Oh, I could, but I just remembered I gotta send an email."

"Go for it. Dammit, I wish we could see Craig, but we don't have a visual on that part of the road. *Or* the mule ranch. Makes me nervous."

"Tell me about it," I said as the Dell booted up. "I'll be much happier when both Craig and Roger join us up here. I'm not cut out for this surveillance crap."

"Surely you jest. You are the snoopiest person I know."

"Snooping and waiting for bad guys to do something awful and not knowing what to do about it, are different."

"True dat. Oh, shit oh, dear! That, rat bastard muleteer is getting into his pickup. And he looks like he's leaving."

"You owe the cuss jar ten dollars. You said the S word."

When we were certain Drew was going out the gate, I abandoned the computer, grabbed the radio, and said, "Earth to R. Incoming. Repeat, incoming."

I received two series of three click spurts as confirmation, then we heard Roger say, "H, going to your rock. C, shelter in place. Confirm."

"Confirm."

"Confirm! Ack! Confirm!"

Jan whirled. "Okay, that's it! Cover for me!" As I moved to the camera just in time to lose sight of Drew's truck, she strode to Trouble's cage and threw a nearby tarp over it. "Noisy little shit—and yes, I know, the cuss jar—is gonna get us busted. Maybe I should take him back to the pickup."

"It'll just be worse, Auntie Jan. At least up here we have *some* control."

"I hope they didn't hear anything down there."

"With all that bird noise? I doubt it."

She took a sweep with the binoculars, then went back to telephoto lens duty. "Uh, *some*one heard. Take a look at this." She moved away from the camera and I took over.

"*Jesus y Maria!* Po Thang's pointing." He was standing motionless, with his snout directed at us, a front paw bent up and his tail skyward. "Crap, he learns one doggie behavior on his own and it's gonna get us murdered."

As I spoke Topaz handed Po Thang a treat to break his concentration. *Where did she get those?* His little doggie brain obviously registered, TREAT! and he relaxed. I laughed, told Jan what happened and asked, "Do you know where the treats came from?"

"Nope, I wondered about that. There's a large box sitting on a shelf near the gate. I figured Drew brought it with the dog food. I guess he can't be *all* bad."

"Oh, yeah?" I grumbled. "Hitler loved his dog."

On that happy note she went back to the camera and I returned to my computer while waiting to hear from Roger or Craig again. I hoped like hell Roger's little B&E job at the mule skinner's house got results. We were flying blind and could use some hard evidence. And a few new, and highly trained recruits to the cause: 'cause I was tired and pissed and a little scared for the outcome.

I got to work on that email and fifteen minutes later I finished my detailed missive as to how we got into this mess, and sent it out, even though I knew the internet was sketchy with only two bars on my jet pack. At least now someone, somewhere, would know where we were. When I closed my laptop, I asked Jan for updates.

"Absolutely nada. Zip. Zilch. Take over, will ya? My teeth are on edge."

As soon as I had camera duty, she stomped to her backpack and pulled out the biggest silver-colored bracelet I'd ever seen. She slipped it on her arm, sat down near me, unscrewed the decorative ball at the top, took a slug from the hole, and handed it to me.

Flask as jewelry? Genius.

Jan with one full of tequila? Priceless.

My radio earbuds crackled.

I hit the transmit button three times, then said, "H."

Three cracks of static told me to wait. Then three more, and I heard, "C."

Craig, Roger and I were all on the radio. We couldn't talk at the same time, so patience was necessary; if one was broadcasting, the others couldn't. I waited *im*patiently.

Finally, Roger said, "C, meet H and J at bird nest. The mule is out of the corral, headed east. Tailing."

"On my way," Craig answered.

"Roger Dodger," I couldn't resist saying.

Jan, who couldn't hear anyone but me asked, "What's up?"

"Seems Drew is on the move, headed east. Roger's following him, and Craig's on his way here."

"Thank goodness. We can use some new company. Can you send Roger a message? Ask him to please send us text updates the first time he gets a good cell signal? Maybe he found clues at Drew's house we can use. I hope that dirty lowdown skunk of a mule skinner isn't just going to the grocery store in Loreto."

"Amen. Texting."

Jan blew a raspberry, then drawled, "So, looks like we get to wait, watch, and chew our nails."

"Yippee, y'all," I said with as much sarcasm as I could conjure, and resumed keeping an eye on Rancho Los Pajaros, albeit somewhat more casually than earlier. Since Drew was not returning to the ranch, I was pretty sure nothing new was going to happen any time soon, and a couple of shots from Jan's bracelet, mixed with whatever was in that pill she gave me, had erased my muscle pain and a good deal of my angst.

Somehow, the spy business seemed a smidge less intense with a buzz on.

"Now I know why those guards down there drink on duty, Miss Jan. And speaking of, we haven't seen the goon Drew shot in the leg, or the one he roughed up for sleeping on the job. So, with Drew headed for who-knows-where, I estimate the bad guy count is down to one able-bodied punk and the truck driver. Who, by the way, is a little old man, but he unloaded heavy boxes like they were empty, so we can't count him out as a threat."

"I can take him," Jan said, fondling a length of rope she'd brought with her.

We work great as an attack team, but I prefer keeping my enemies at gun's length, while Jan wants to lasso and truss them up like a Thanksgiving turkey, maybe breaking a wing or two in the process.

"No doubt you could, but he might be a handful. I didn't see a gun on him, but older Mexicans do tend to carry machetes. And he's got that wiry look of a farmer or fisherman. Someone who's worked hard physically his whole life."

"And now he's a smuggler."

"Yes, but I noticed how gently he handled the birds and girls. And I caught him frowning at those young punks with obvious disgust a couple of times. He might prove an ally."

Jan brightened. "You think so? We could sure use someone on the inside right now. Or, we need Nacho."

"Already sent him the whole story."

"What? When?"

"I told you I was sending a couple of emails."

"I thought you meant to your parents or something."

"Jan, you know my parents refuse to do anything electronic."

"So, now Nacho knows where we are and what we're doing?"

"If he opens his email, he does."

"That's a big if, Hetta. Anything Nacho gets from you he tends to trash, lest he gets dragged into one of your debacles."

I shrugged. "True, but Nacho owes us one. He dragged *us* into the French kidnapping mess."

"True dat. Who else did you copy?"

"Rhonda. I asked her to forward my email to Cholo, that mysterious Mexican seal-type dude who may or may not be her amour. He'd come in right handy about now."

"Cholo! Oh yes, he'd do serious damage to these amateurs. However, my guess is we'll wrap this up today all by ourselves."

I gave Jan the squint eye, checking for any sign the tequila was messing with her judgement.

"Miz Jan, might I remind you we have no guns, and there are only three of us. Four counting Topaz, but she's locked up and in no position to do a damned thing to help anyone right now. How do you figure we can wrap this up today?"

"Optimism."

"Yeah, tequila does that for me, as well."

Chapter Twenty-two

CRAIG RADIOED US once he was parked next to my pickup, and Jan went down the path to lead him up to our bivouac, as we were now calling it.

"Hey, Craig, you didn't by any chance bring a pizza, did you?" I asked, when he crested the hill. I gave him a hug and was privately annoyed that he wasn't even breathing hard.

He stepped back and sniffed. "You two have been into the rum ration, right?"

Damned teetotalers; they can smell alcohol at thirty paces.

Despite being covered, Trouble squawked, "Tequila!"

"Shut up, bird. Just a wee dram to calm our shredded nerves, mind ye," I said in my best Oliver Twist accent. "Please, sir, could I have more?"

Craig laughed. "Right now I wish I'd never quit drinking. My nerves could stand a hit, but *one* of us must stay sober. Have you heard anything from Roger yet?"

"No. He'll have to stop to text, or at least wait until

he gets off the windy road down to Mex One at Loreto."

"What's been going on below?"

"Check it out for yourself. They're down to two goons and an old truck driver right now. I wish we could get a message to Topaz. She needs to make a break for it while Drew's gone. He's obviously the brains in the operation."

"How can we do that?" he asked.

"Hell, I don't know. I was hoping you'd have an idea. I'm suffering burn out."

"Ack! Tequila!"

Jan jabbed a finger at Trouble. "You want the tarp back?"

"What kind of lock is on that aviary gate?" Craig asked.

"It used to be just a drop bar, but who knows by now? That rat bastard, Drew, ain't no idiot."

He made some adjustments to the telephoto lens. "I'm gonna zero in, see what I can see."

I watched him as he handled Roger's huge camera with ease, removing it from the tripod and holding it in one large hand. It took two of us to even set it on the tripod and dog it down. Now that my giant of a friend had it, he deftly made adjustments.

"I think I see the old man. Or at least his sandals and tattered pants legs. Looks like he's taking a siesta in the bed of a yellow truck."

"That'd be he. The others are wearing new jeans."

Trouble, for some reason started barking. Jan threw the tarp over the cage, but it was too late.

"Uh-oh, ladies. Po Thang is barking at us."

"Topaz will calm him down. She knows we're up here, or at least I hope she does. Like I said before, I know if I were in her little boots I'd feel better knowing that friendlies were watching over me. Not that we can do squat, at least until Roger returns. With four of us, I think we can pull off a sneak attack after dark."

"*If* the other two guards are out of commission."

"Hetta thinks the truck driver might help us."

"Really? Why?"

I told him my observations where the old man was concerned. "Just my opinion. I could be wrong."

"Did Hetta Coffey just say she might be wrong?" Jan cackled.

Craig chuckled. "I do believe she did."

"Bite me!"

"Bite me!" Trouble shrieked, despite the tarp. Then he began barking again, sounding for all the world like Po Thang.

"Oh, hell, an armed guard just came out of the house and is looking this way."

"Jan, grab that bird and shut him up! If you have to, take him down the path toward the pickup so the sound won't carry."

"Check!"

I grabbed the binoculars to give Craig an extra set of eyes. The surly guard was stalking toward the bird enclosure, yelling so loud we could hear him. "*¡Pinche chucho! Callate!*" He raised the gun barrel as he closed on the gate, then stopped and took aim at Po Thang and

Topaz. My heart seized, and I gasped.

"What? What's happening?" Jan yelled as she shoved Trouble into an empty cooler and sat on it.

Evidently the goon calling Po Thang an effing mutt, and demanding he shut up, just didn't resonate. Back hair up, teeth bared, ears back, Po Thang was the very picture of menace. He charged the chain link fencing, sending the guard scampering backward. The man lost his balance and fell on his designer-jeaned ass.

Topaz tackled Po Thang and got him in a headlock, but he was so worked up, I was afraid he might bite her in his attempt to get loose and attack the guard. Never mind he hadn't figured out there was a fence between them. In one practiced move, Topaz pulled off the bandana she wore as a head band, muzzled Po Thang, and lay across him.

The guard scrambled to his feet and picked up his gun, which looked more like a semi-automatic than an automatic, but either was deadly at close range. If he started shooting into the pen, it would be a massacre.

The old man nimbly slid from the truck bed, yelled loudly, ran toward the guard, and the punk spun to face him. As he did so, he tried to swing the gun barrel at the driver and fell against the aviary gate.

Topaz dropped him where he stood.

Pandemonium broke out in the cage as birds screeched, girls squealed in fear, and the old man froze in his tracks, staring in disbelief at Topaz and the still form on the ground.

Jan was pitching a hissy fit next to me, jerking on my

arm while demanding to know what was going on. She let go and yelled, "Oh, shit! Was that a gunshot?"

"You betchum! Topaz just nailed a guard. Oh, hell, here come the other *Pendejos*. Two of 'em!"

I watched in horror as the goons, one of them still bloodied from his earlier ass stomping, and the other limping, ran from the house. Luckily, only one of them was able to carry a gun.

"Those bastards are charging the pen, and they're still out of Topaz's range!" My voice was up at least three octaves, I could barely catch my breath, and my heart was practically jumping out of my chest. All remnants of the pill and tequila disappeared as my stomach went cold. "Jan! Let Trouble loose."

Jan didn't hesitate. I knew my parrot would leap into the fray, and hoped turning Trouble loose on the men below would at least create a diversion, but he did better than that. Drawn to the brouhaha below, he soared down the mountain like Mighty Mouse, covering the distance in a flash. Then he aimed his entire twenty or so ounces of heft at the lead man—the one with a gun—who never knew what hit him.

The goon screamed and grabbed the top of his bloodied head with both hands as Trouble sailed out of sight, and to the safety of some tall trees.

During the confusion that followed, the old man snatched up the dead guard's long gun and handed it to Topaz through the feeder gate. She let go of Po Thang, took aim, and evidently ordered the old man to hit the ground for he dropped like a rock. The moment he was out of harm's way, she easily finished off the two *Pendejos*. Seconds later, she and Po Thang were free.

Jan wrested the binoculars from my death grip on them and said, "Hetta, you better calm down before you have a danged stoke!"

I forced myself to take deep Yoga breaths while she gave me a running report.

"Looks like an all-clear. The driver is opening the gate to the aviary. Jeez I hope Po Thang doesn't eat him. Craig, you haven't said a word. You got all this?"

"On video. We better get down there as fast as we can."

"Hetta, you okay to take over up here?"

"Hell no! I want to hug my dog, now!"

"Po Thang is fine." She handed me the binoculars. "See for yourself."

Topaz was body checking the three thugs, Po Thang on her heels sniffing the dead men nervously from a safe distance.

She started to walk away but turned on her heel and frisked the dude Drew shot the day before, and she'd just put out of his misery. She pulled her cellphone from his pocket, tried to turn it on and gave us a thumb's down sign. No service, of course.

The truck driver ushered the girls out of the cage one at a time to keep birds from escaping with them. He gently guided the upset children to the truck, patting them on the back as he did so.

While I watched, Topaz gave us a two-thumbs up, hand-signed they were gonna roll, and we'd meet down the road. Trouble sat in her bushy hair, preening and singing.

I made one quick call to Roger while I still had service, left him a messaged update on our much-improved situation, and told him we planned to head for Loreto ASAP. Craig volunteered to lug the camera equipment down the hill, so Jan and I could intercept the taco truck. We would rendezvous at Mission San Javier, so if he saw Drew coming our way, he could stop him. We didn't ask how, nor did we care.

Unless there was a miracle of some kind, I knew Jan and I would be out of any manner of contact with either Craig or Roger for at least an hour. My fingers and toes were mentally crossed against the possibility Drew had somehow eluded Roger and was in our area again.

As we sped toward Rancho Los Pajaros —and a rendezvous with Topaz—we were flying blind, hard information-wise.

"Hetta, are you still holdin' your breath? That why your knuckles are white?"

I exhaled tequila-laced air and relaxed my death-grip on the steering wheel. "I can't help worrying about where that dirty rotten mule-skinner is."

"Me too. I can't wait to get my hands on him."

"I *meant* I was afraid we wouldn't get safely to Loreto before *he* finds *us*."

"I wouldn't fret much about that, if I were you. When they left the bird sanctuary, Topaz and Po Thang were riding shotgun in the taco truck. And now she has an arsenal she lifted off those thugs."

"Yabbut—look! There they are!" A cloud of dust was headed our way. "At least I hope it's them. Should we hide, just in case?"

Jan scanned the desert. Not a boulder, bush or tree in sight. "Unless we turn tail for the boulder field, we're plumb outta luck, Chica. Just stop. If it's not them, we'll know soon enough. What's the worst thing that can happen?"

"Topaz could shoot us?"

"And me, flat out of white flags. Put your emergency lights on. Topaz'll hopefully recognize your pickup through all this dust before she starts slingin' lead."

Despite the tense situation we burst into sniggers.

The flatbed truck topped a grade and ground out of sight again into a *vado*—a dry creek—but at least we knew it was them. They spotted us, as well, and started honking.

As soon as we drew side by side, Topaz let Po Thang out, and he enthusiastically almost flattened me in the dirt. As Jan rushed to hug Topaz, Trouble circled overhead, scolding us with that annoying, "Ack! Ack! Ack!"

The truck driver watched the scene with wide eyes, shook his head, and left the driver's seat. He opened the canvas and waved the girls out. They were hesitant until they saw Topaz, Jan, and me jumping up and down and squealing like teenagers.

"Okay, everyone," Topaz said in Spanish. "We gotta go! Load up. Hetta, you take the lead. Jan, you ride with her. Let's get the hell out of here."

"Just a second. Did you see Anna and Humberto? They were the caretakers at Rancho Los Pajaros?"

"No, the house was empty. I opened every door and gave it a quick search. And Po Thang was with me, so I think he would have sniffed them out." She turned to the truck driver and asked him about them in Spanish. He shook his head. "No, *señorita*."

"Crap! I was hoping they were with you guys."

"Hetta, we'll find them. For now, we have to roll."

"I know. Is the driver going with us?"

"I gave him the option of walking back to the bird sanctuary and telling Drew, when he returns, that he was attacked and the hostages were taken away in his truck, but he wants to come with us. Right, *señor*?"

The old man smiled, showing a lot of gum. "How could I leave? I am surrounded by beautiful women. Let us go," he said, in almost perfect English. We took turns pecking his cheeks, making him glow with pleasure.

Turns out his name is Eli Garza, and he was born and raised in San Diego.

Chapter Twenty-three

JAN AND I were belted in and ready to drive the lead vehicle to Loreto when Topaz hefted two AK47's, with several extra banana mags, through the window. "I made a withdrawal from Mr. Muleshoe's arsenal. A gal just can't have too many guns these days, right?"

"Oooh," I cooed. "I almost hope someone tries to make our day!"

With Jan and Topaz riding shotgun in our vehicles, we slowly drove into the main plaza at Mission San Javier. It was devoid of people, with only an old dog lying on a bench, trying to catch the last rays of the sun. He opened one eye and went back to sleep.

Craig waited for us behind a building off the main plaza, as he told us when we were within VHF radio range. He was doing his best to blend in, which was a little difficult in his case; the locals, had there been any, might have figured a tall black cowboy just might not be from around these parts.

I rushed over to him, eager to know if he'd talked to

Roger since we left the bivouac.

"Nope. No luck so far. He must still be on Drew's tail, but I'm only getting one bar, so I can't talk to him."

Checking my phone I sighed in resignation. "Oh, well. We'll pick up cell service down the road. I know the perfect spot. Meanwhile, you have to meet some folks. Follow me."

We introduced him to the driver, then pulled up the rollup canvas on his truck. When they saw Craig, two of the youngest looked like they might faint, but his gentle voice, smooth Spanish, and large grin won them over. Even so, when we walked away, we heard one ask the other if Craig was their new owner. It broke my heart. And made Jan furious. I was almost sorry for Drew when we caught up to him. Okay, NOT!

We'd given Topaz a VHF radio and Jan's cellphone, so we had plenty of ways to communicate if need be. I took the lead again, with a now-armed Craig bringing up the rear as we made for Loreto. Despite the paved road, the going was slow.

Twice we encountered other vehicles, but they looked to be ranchers. Kids hunkered in the backs of their pickups, along with a dog or two, and Mexican plastic totes, most likely filled with groceries and supplies, were piled high. We waved, they waved, and we went our separate ways.

As we topped a hill, right before the low water crossing where I'd spent the night, all of our phones started dinging. I looked back to see Topaz waggling hers out the window, so I pulled over as far as I could and the convoy halted. No one got out immediately, as we were checking our messages.

Craig was the first to let out a whoop and come charging toward the truck. Jan, Topaz and I jumped out to meet him, all of us grinning ear to ear. Not only had he talked to Roger, he actually had some good news for a change. "Roger's got a pretty good handle on the operation now, and he'll fill us in when he meets us at the house in Loreto."

We were speculating on Roger's brief report when one of the girls leaned through a split in the canvas and asked, timidly, if they could get out. Craig walked to the back and helped each one down, lifting them gently, as if they weighed almost nothing, which most of them did.

We walked with them to a place out of view of the road and the men, where we could all relieve ourselves in privacy. One of the girls whispered something to Topaz, who gave me a look, pressed her lips together, and patted the girl's skinny shoulder.

"What's up?" I asked.

"They want to know what we're going to do with them, Chica"

"We let them go, that's what."

Topaz shook that mane of hers. "Not that easy. They're children. Not one of them is even eighteen. And they're from the mainland."

"So what *do* we do with them?"

"Danged if I know. Back in Arizona it wouldn't be a problem, there are agencies to handle this kind of situation, but here in Mexico? And let's not forget they witnessed me offing those goons at the bird sanctuary. Let's just take it one step at a time, then get this bunch off the mountain and safe."

"To?"

"Loreto."

"To?"

"Our rental house. Where else?"

"Hoo-boy, I'll let you handle that witch who owns the house. She blew a gasket when we brought in Craig and Roger, and now we're housing an extra ten girls and an old man."

"She's not the owner, she's the caretaker. Trust me, if we pay her under the table, she'll love it."

"Love might be a stretch, but you deal with her, okay?"

"When did you get to be such a wuss?"

"Sorry, I'm just plumb wore out."

"You're tired? I spent the night in a birdcage. I'm covered in droppings, and I've eaten nothing but overripe fruit for two days. Uh, have you got any Imodium?"

I patted her shoulder. "Soldier up, copper. Oh, and stay downwind, will ya?"

Luckily, the rental house had its own drive-in courtyard, with plenty of parking spaces. Even then, we left the truck on the street and spirited the girls inside under cover of dark. Roger, who was waiting for us when we pulled up to the house, figured a flatbed in the driveway might be a little much for our hostess, who lived right down the street.

We'd barely gotten the girls inside when she rang the doorbell repeatedly.

Po Thang and Trouble raised holy hell, and Topaz signaled she'd go out and talk to the woman. Roger handed her a fistful of cash before she went out the door, and within minutes all was well.

"What'd she say?" Jan asked. "She was pretty adamant about the number of people in the house."

Topaz laughed. "Look at me. I'm covered in bird shit and feathers. Would you argue with me?"

"Hell no! Please, Topaz, hit the shower while we sort out sleeping spaces."

"Who wants carnitas?" Craig asked.

Like, everyone!

While Craig and Roger drove into town for carnitas and to return the dusty rental cars before the agency closed, we raided closets for sheets, blankets, and the like. And we all took turns in the shower, depleting the hot water before I got my turn, of course.

The guys returned with huge bags of food, and several sacks of girls' clothing they bought at a second-hand shop. The girls went into a bedroom, threw their miniskirts, high heels and crop tops out the door, and emerged dressed like schoolgirls, in plaid uniforms.

"Hey, Roger," Jan teased, "who knew you were such a fashionista? You a Brittany Spears fan?"

Craig laughed. "Hey! There's a method to his madness. We can't just go driving down Mex 1, through at least two military stops, with a carload of underaged hooker lookalikes. So, let me introduce you to the schoolmistress who is taking her girls on a field trip." He hooked a thumb at Topaz, who was dressed in sweats. Her wet hair was corralled by a towel turban.

"Tell me your brilliant plan later. Let's eat!"

I'd laid out our dinner buffet in the kitchen and we devoured plates piled high with carnitas, beans, and tortillas like we'd never eat again.

The girls ate in silence, only looking up to smile shyly at Craig occasionally. Po Thang had cozied up to Topaz, who was sneaking him carnitas, even though Craig was frowning at the idea.

Catching his disapproval, Topaz asked, "What? You try eating old fruit for two days. He *deserves* carnitas."

"Woof."

"Didn't I see him getting treats and canned dog food?" Jan asked.

"Yes, but he wouldn't share."

That got a laugh, then I said, "So, Drew sells young girls into slavery and smuggles exotic birds, but makes sure the dog gets fed? What's with that?"

No one had a comment.

Trouble flew to Topaz's shoulder and she waved him off. "No way, bird. I've had it with your kind for some time to come."

"Ack! Ack! Ack!"

Chapter Twenty-four

AFTER OUR MOB of guests was fed and put to bed, we all settled into the living area for a complete Roger report.

Jan and I commandeered the couch and sank down with our after dinner beers. My head lolled back on a stack of cushions and Jan was fighting to stay alert, as well.

"I know we're all bushed," Roger said, "but we gotta talk. I already filled Craig in on the latest when we went for carnitas. In a nutshell, there's a smallish ship at Puerto Escondido, waiting to take the birds north."

Jan and I un-slouched, all ears. "Wow, that's a bombshell. Tell us all!" Jan said.

"Okay, as you know, Drew went straight from his mule ranch to Puerto Escondido, and I tailed him like I said I was gonna do. I wasn't worried about losing him, cuz he stopped for gas in Loreto, and while he was in the gentleman's room I stuck a GPS tracker on his pickup."

"He ain't no gentleman," Jan growled.

"Hush, I want to hear the whole story. Go on, Roger," I urged.

"Anyhow, he parked near a long concrete dock close to where a bunch of boats were anchored."

I nodded. "Us boaters call that anchorage the Waiting Room. I know it well. What kind of boat is at the *muelle?*"

"It looks like a small shrimper, or maybe a crew boat for the shrimp fleet. Maybe forty, forty-five feet. I didn't worry too much about being spotted, cuz the danged thing was lit up like a Mississippi party boat, and they were blasting Mexican rap. No crew in sight. Drew entered the bridge by a side door, and I could clearly see him greeting a man. So I listened."

I put my beer down and glared at him. "You went aboard? All we need is for you to get snatched like Topaz did."

Topaz, who had been listening intently, rolled her eyes at me. "I didn't get snatched." All heads turned in her direction, and she shrugged. "I *wanted* in."

I was nonplussed. "You got my dog kidnapped on *purpose?* What if they'd shot him?"

"I had your gun, remember? If I thought they were going to harm him, or me, I'd have unloaded on Drew so fast he'd never know what hit him. Those other fools were no contest. Besides, we needed Agent Thang and his critter cam to ID the head dude later."

"The critter cam! I'd forgotten all about it in the excitement." I called Po Thang over, took off his harness, and removed the chip from the tiny camera. "We can look at this later if we need to. I figure it ran out of batteries about twelve hours ago, which is a good thing cuz the last thing we need is a video of Topaz shooting up the compound. Agents Dawg and Topaz, you done good."

Po Thang shook, grinned his goofy golden grin, and climbed up on the couch. I shoved him off. "Not *that* good."

"Can we get back on track here?" Roger asked. "I need some sleep."

"Amen. So, if you didn't go aboard, how did you listen to the conversation between what may be the captain and Drew inside that boat?" I asked.

"Oh, he's the captain, all right. His boat's named *Doña Esperanza*, home port is Guaymas. And I didn't need to go on the boat, I eavesdropped from my car."

"Oh, come on," Jan scoffed. "Hetta can hear a gnat land, but she ain't that good."

"I used my Uzi."

What? "You got a gun that listens?"

Roger reached over, rummaged in his large canvas bag and pulled out a high tech looking device. "Ladies and germs, I give you the Uzi Observation Parabolic Sound Device UZIOD1s!"

"Wow," seemed the operative word.

"She's trigger-activated, eight X monocular view finder, and comes with a built in recorder. A must have for covert work."

He handed the Uzi to Jan, who cuddled it like she would a baby. That girl dearly loves snoop toys. "It's so light!"

"Under thirty ounces."

"How far can it snoop?"

"Three hundred feet. Wanna hear the playback?"

You bet your sweet bippy we did.

Gathering around Roger, we watched as he fast-forwarded through some boggles and scraping sounds, then we saw the two men talking in the glassed in bridge. "Turn up the volume," Jan said. "I ain't Hetta, you know."

I was not at the top of my game, either. I could clearly hear, but the conversation was in speedy Spanish. Mine is passable, but once they go into overdrive I only catch every few words. However, knowing the context helped.

When the recording and video ended with Drew leaving the boat, I asked for a full translation, because as far as I could tell, there was no mention of any girls, only birds.

Topaz volunteered as translator, answering my question about the white slavery thing. "They never discussed the girls, but they plan to start transporting and loading the birds tomorrow night, one truckload at a time. Tough patooties, huh? We've got the Pendejo's truck."

That got a laugh.

Roger said, "We could return it before he gets back."

Everyone looked at him like he'd been smoking funny cigarettes.

"Oh, sure, Rog. Just drive right back into that debacle we left behind? '*Hola* there, Drew, *mi amigo,* I bring you *trucke* back,'" Topaz said with exaggerated Spanglish, sounding like Sofía Vergara.

"Okay, put that way it sounds ridiculous, but I'd bet my Stetson he didn't go back up the mountain tonight. Turns out he's got a lady friend stashed here in town, and he's at her place right now. Or at least he was when Craig and I drove by when we went for carnitas. You know, he probably shouldn't leave his fancy pickup parked on the street like that. Vandals have no respect. I guarantee you the flatbed could beat him back to the old rancho."

I groaned inwardly. The idea of going back up there for any reason gave me a stomach ache. "Why should we provide the mule skinner a means to move the birds?"

"Because we *know* what his plan is for them. When, and where. If he has to start from scratch, so do we."

Jan nodded. "Hate to say it, but it makes sense. We'll be all over his every move."

"If someone will follow me, I'll take the truck back and drop it off," Topaz said.

I shook my head. "No way, girl. If by some chance you didn't get out in time, he'd probably shoot you on sight, what with you leaving his men full of holes and his hostages missing."

Roger held up his hands. "Here's the way I see it. Drew returns, finds the place in ruins, but there's the truck, still sitting there. He'll just have to do everything himself since he doesn't have any help, and it'll slow him down some."

"Or," I said, "he brings in a new crew of thugs. We sure as hell don't want that."

"*Señora*, I will return the truck and help him load the birds."

We all turned to see Eli, the truck driver, who we thought to be asleep, standing at the foot of the stairs.

I shook my head. "No, Don Eli, it is too dangerous. He might blame you."

Topaz and the old man exchanged a look. "We left no witnesses," she said.

What the hell; the 'no witnesses' thing, in this case, worked fine for me.

Roger scanned the room for comments, and when none were offered, he said, "Okay, then. Way I see it, if Don Eli is willin' to go back, he can 'discover' the crime scene and wait for Drew."

"Where was Don Eli when the so-called crime occurred? He better have a danged good story?"

"Good point, Hetta."

Eli took off his sombrero and pointed to the top of his head, and the bloody slash there. "I was grazed by a bullet that came from nowhere, and never saw what happened until I woke up. I was shocked by the carnage, but waited for the boss to return. After all, the birds do need someone to care for them."

"Okay then," Roger said. 'My bet is the lowlife will most likely cut his losses and start loading birds for tomorrow's drop at the ship. Or Eli could open the cage and just let them go, but Craig vetoed that."

Craig, who hadn't said much, nodded. "It would kill most of them. They're from down south, and without the cover afforded by the cage and tarps, they'll die."

Topaz agreed. "That's why I didn't leave the cage open. They have enough food and water for at least a day or so. They're fine for now. Where do you figure the boat intends to take them?"

"My guess?" Roger said. "Northern Sonora, off-load the cages to some beach and move them to another hiding place of some sort. And from there cross the border with drug mules, or whatever works to get 'em into the States. There are news stories every day about lion and tiger cubs, and birds of all sorts, being found at border crossings. Heaven knows how many get through."

"Then we gotta be on those birds like Hetta on a carrot cake," Jan said.

I shot her a middle digit. "Sonora is just covered with ranches and farms. There must be thousands of places to stash contraband. And the smuggling routes are already well established by cartels, and secured by gangs."

Roger nodded. "That corridor is busier than an LA freeway at rush hour. But we'll track them carefully, one way or another. With that in mind, everyone think about it and we'll talk tomorrow. Let's get Don Eli on the road, and then I'm going to bed."

"Will you be okay to travel tonight? You are not too tired?" I asked the old man.

"No problem, *señorita*. I slept most of the morning until *señorita* Topaz began shooting everyone. She is my kind of woman."

Chapter Twenty-five

WHILE THE OLD man gathered his bedroll, I packed him a sack of leftover carnitas, beans and tortillas, and stuck in a roll of two hundred peso notes. Also, I didn't want him to leave without knowing more about him. Was he brave, or did he have other motives in mind?

As we walked out to the truck, I asked, "Did you grow up in the States? Your English is excellent."

"Yes. My parents walked across the border back when you could do that easily, and I was born a year later. They worked the fields in the Imperial Valley, and so did I when I was old enough." He grinned, "Meaning five or six, in those days."

"And now you live in Mexico?"

"Cheaper here. My social security goes a lot farther."

"You're collecting Social Security?"

He laughed. "You think I'm not old enough, or not qualified?"

That flustered me. Anything I said would sound judgmental, so—uncharacteristically—I clammed up.

"Sorry, I was teasing you. I received my green card

because of the Reagan amnesty. I had no birth certificate. I was born in a shack in the fields, and never went to a real school. My mother taught me at night, after work. When I found jobs as an adult, I paid into a false Social Security account for years, so I was finally given credit for the money I paid, and then, twenty years and many lawyers later, I became a legal American citizen."

"And moved to Mexico. You have dual citizenship?"

"Yes. Here I can live comfortably, and even make extra money."

"Let me guess. This is your truck."

"Yes. I was hired to haul a load of fruit to Rancho Los Pajaros."

"And the girls?"

He bowed his head and said, very quietly, "On my mother's honor, I did not know they were in the truck. And there were always birds around, I thought they were being rescued. Until the *pendejos* showed up."

"I figured that. You looked shocked when you saw the children."

"You were watching?"

Not willing to give up all my spying secrets, I said, "Yes, and I told Jan we could probably rely on you because of the way you treated the girls and frowned at the punks."

"They are vermin. I stayed because I was so concerned about the birds, and then this small woman and a dog were captured. I had to stay."

"Did you, by any chance, see my friends, Humberto and Anna?"

"I have known them for a long time, and Drew told me they went to live with their children in La Paz. I was happy for them. They love spending time with the grandchildren."

And you believed him? I wanted to ask but didn't. Why upset him now?

"I have grandchildren, as well," he continued. "I could not leave those *niñas* to their fate. Even though Drew warned his men to leave the girls alone, I did not trust them. I have granddaughters their age. Babies! Miss Topaz has been talking to them. They trust her. One of them is just turned thirteen. The oldest is seventeen. Someone is missing them."

"Then you joined the right team. We'll make sure they're safe, and with any luck, put the likes of Drew out of business."

"God willing, *señora*."

"Please, call me Hetta, or Café. And by the way, it is *señorita*."

He brightened. "Really? I have this son...just kidding again."

"*Hasta luego. Que le vaya bien,*" I told him, as he climbed into his truck after we gave it a good going over to make sure there was no evidence against him for Drew to find.

Heroes come in different forms.

I slept like I'd had a shot of morphine. I don't think I moved all night, or what was left of it, when I finally crashed. By the time I stumbled downstairs, it was eight o'clock and Jan was whipping up breakfast for the girls while they watched cartoons on American cable TV. I guess the Disney language is universal, for they were giggling.

Roger, Craig, and Topaz were nowhere to be seen.

"About time, your laziness," Jan quipped. "Coffee's brewed. You want pancakes?"

"You're offering me devil food?"

"You've earned it just this once. So, want some?"

"Naw, just coffee, and lots of it. Where's the rest of the team?"

"Scouting. They couldn't resist going in to town to watch Drew's reaction when he found all his tires flat this morning. They should be back shortly, and we'll formalize a game plan. Have you thought about one?"

"Not unless I dreamed it. I did have a nice talk with Eli last night before he left. He's not at all what I first thought of him. I just hope he doesn't get harmed in any way for his heroism."

Jan smartly flipped a hotcake. "Topaz gave him a gold star, as well. It's amazing the people you meet down here. It's so easy to pigeonhole them, and then you get a grand surprise. Like, who knew Meghan Markle's father lives in Rosarita?"

"Hell, I didn't even know who Meghan Markle was until she snagged Prince Harry." I moved my nose closer to the cooktop. "Okay, just one pancake."

She started plating and called the girls to come and get it. They quickly returned to the television. I shook away the image of what might have become of them. I'd seen the boney, hollow-eyed young women in Cannes. Oh, wait, those were models.

Jan sat with me while I crammed pancakes into my mouth. They were perfectly cooked, light and fluffy. "You think Eli will be safe with Drew? Guy's a loose cannon. Shooting and roughing up half your team ain't what I'd call good people skills."

"Ha! There's the pot calling the kettle black. You, of all people, should be able to relate, Miz Hetta."

"Oh, hush. Roger's background check on mule dude unearthed some drug and anger management issues. I wouldn't want to be there when he discovers all his guys tits-up, and the girls long gone."

"No, but it might be worth the climb to our bivouac to watch."

"Are you serious?"

"Hell, no!"

Topaz and the girls left for La Paz a little before noon in a van Roger rented.

Jan and I, in my pickup, followed. We left Jan's Jeep with Roger and Craig.

Luckily, in the Baja, it wasn't abnormal to see way more people than the law allowed crammed into small vans, so schoolgirls packed in like sardines for a field trip wouldn't raise any eyebrows.

"You think she'll have any trouble at the military stops?" I asked Jan. "What if they want the girls' IDs or something?"

"I doubt it. If Topaz tells the army guys, if they even

stop her, that she's taking the girls to the orphanage in La Paz, they won't think it's anything unusual. She's schooled the girls to giggle and sing when approaching an installation. Besides, going south, they rarely even look at anyone."

"Everyone knows it's not a real orphanage, anyhow. Just kids who live there because there are no high schools nearby, and they stay there during the school year."

"But," I said, "there's a high school in Loreto."

"Most of these guys at the check points are from the mainland. Chances are they won't know or care about that. Just in case, though, Topaz is ready for them with a spiel about there not being a *Catholic* high school in Loreto."

"I thought I saw one."

"Jeez, Hetta. Would you try and think positive here?"

"Okay, okay. You know I'm a worrywart. Now that we have time to discuss the subject seriously, just what the heck are we going to do with those kids? It's fine for them to crash at Rhonda's condo for a day or two, but then we have to find someone to take them in until they can contact their families."

"We'll stick Topaz with the girls, and we'll deal with Drew. We'll want to beat feet back to the B team as soon as possible."

The checkpoints, as we hoped, were no problemo. The Mexican military are looking for guns and drugs, and the occasional cold Coke on a hot day. I also carry packages of cookies and candy, but never pass them out until I've been waved through. Heaven forbid it look like I'm trying to perpetrate a bribe. Most of the soldiers are teenaged grunts from southern Mexico, and their service is mandatory. They are paid almost nothing, and any treats are very welcome.

We went straight to Rhonda's condo in La Paz to get the girls and Topaz settled in. If they'd had pajamas, it would look like a giant sleepover. The girls were used to bedding down on dirt floors, so carpeting would be a luxury.

I opened the door to the condo with the girls, Topaz, and Jan right on my heels. When I stepped into the darkened interior, I stopped in my tracks. From my left, I heard the distinctive sound of a round being chambered. Stepping back, I knocked my girl scout troop into the hallway.

Hitting the deck, I drew my .380 and rolled, aiming in the direction of the noise, and yelled, "Freeze, *Pendejo!*"

And that's how I ended up in a Mexican standoff with a very large and dangerous looking man.

"Hetta? I thought you were in Loreto." Cholo stood and peered around me, trying to see into the hallway. "What is all that noise?"

"Screaming teenagers, and if you don't drop that big honking gun I'm going to turn them loose on you."

Cholo grinned, showing off perfect white teeth against his dark skin. He gently laid down his Springfield XDM, overacting as he did his best to look frightened. Clasping his hands on his head, he continued to grin. "I surrender! Teenagers, they terrify me. However, Hetta, that weapon of yours? What is it? A Chihuahua 5000? With a bark worse than its bite?

I was tempted to shoot him smack dab in his own Chihuahua for making fun of my gun.

Chapter Twenty-six

ABOUT CHOLO: Jan, Rhonda, and I met him in Cannes, aboard a large yacht we were staying on.

The reason why we were there is a little convoluted, but let's just say we were already in France, a young Mexican girl had vanished, and we were involved in the team commissioned to find her at the request of her grandfather. During our time on board, Cholo and Rhonda got chummy. The next thing we know they were an item in La Paz.

And he was just the dude we needed to help us with the situation we found ourselves embroiled in, despite his dissing my gun.

If the teens were fascinated with Craig, Cholo—with his dark, stern face, thick, black, military cut hair, and resemblance to a handsome, stone-faced, Mayan version of the Incredible Hulk—sent them over the moon. He was a compadre of Nacho's, who is mine and Jan's mystery Mexican. We think. Like Cholo, we have no idea who Nacho is, or who he works for.

The tittering, giggling, and eye-cuts at Cholo soon

tried our patience, and Topaz banished our teenyboppers to the master bedroom, loaded up with huge bags of potato chips and cokes. She showed them how to use the remote on Rhonda's sixty-inch TV and left them to it. We thought they would enjoy all the Spanish language channels, but from the sounds of it, they soon found English language cartoons.

We mixed adult beverages from Rhonda's bar and sat down to get caught up on who knew what.

"Rhonda's message said you were trying to save some endangered birds, and that someone was holding your friend and dog hostage along with the birds, and some girls. So, I see you have the girls."

"That was me, Cholo. Po Thang and I escaped with the young ladies. I've heard a lot about you," Topaz told him.

"And I have heard almost nothing about *you*."

"She's a — "

Topaz cut me off. "A good friend from Arizona. I thought I was coming to Mexico for a vacation. Some vacation!" She gave me a meaningful look from under those poufy bangs of hers. Meaning, *Shut the hell up. I don't want this guy to know I'm a cop.*

Cholo tilted his head. "And yet you managed to escape, all on your own?"

"Oh, no. There was this nice old man who let us go. We just sneaked out and Hetta found us."

He smiled. His eyes didn't. "So you say. But, that is done. What is the present situation, other than we have a bedroom full of giggling little girls?"

Po Thang had sidled over, rested his chin on Cholo's large thigh, and was giving him adoring looks. But then again, the big man had a potato chip bag in his hand. He gave one to my dog, who eagerly waited for another. "No," he said, "no more. They are not healthy for you." Po Thang groaned and lay down.

Why does my dog obey everyone but me?

Jan was giving Cholo a blow-by-blow rundown of what happened at Rancho Los Pajaros, albeit an edited one that didn't include Topaz shooting her way out with my Chihuahua 5000 and a couple of commandeered assault rifles.

"So, now the boat waits at Puerto Escondido and your friends are watching it?" he asked.

"Yes. They think it will take at least three days to load the birds, then the boat will deliver them to the mainland. Probably Sonora."

"But this mule person. His operation has now been compromised."

I shrugged. "We figure he'll cut his losses and go with the bird plan already in place."

"And what do you want to do about it?"

Jan indignantly huffed, "Obviously we want to save the birds. And then remove his *huevos*."

Cholo grinned. "And how do you plan to execute this operation?"

"Honestly," I said. "We haven't exactly figured that one out. But if they offload the birds on a Sonoran beach, they must have a place to put them until they can be smuggled into the US, right?"

"You are making a lot of assumptions. How did you reach the conclusion that the birds will be taken to Sonora?"

"The boat is from Sonora. There are miles of deserted beaches up north, and the state is pretty much agricultural. It's a perfect place to hide a bunch of birds."

"Name of the boat?" Cholo was beginning to sound like a television cop.

"*Doña Esperanza*, home port is Guaymas"

He nodded and pulled out his cellphone. "I must make a phone call. Would you pick up some food from downstairs?"

"They deliver," I said.

"I do not wish any strangers at the door."

"Gee, I have this great idea," Jan snipped. "Why don't I pick up some food from downstairs?" She simpered and asked Cholo, "You want some fries with that, Sweetcakes?"

He shook his head and sighed. "*Gringas!*"

A Mexican to-go order is never simple. When you order tacos, you end up with another large bag of cucumber slices, salsa—at least three kinds, all hot—shredded cabbage, jalapeño peppers, hot pickled veggies, guacamole sauce, tortilla chips and *pico de gallo*. An order of thirty-five tacos with an order of fries—I always get an extra taco or two for Po Thang—took quite some time, and both of us to heft our dinner upstairs.

After dinner we called Roger and Craig, who were staked out near the dock at Puerto Escondido, waiting for the first load of birds to arrive. They said they'd text when it did.

Cholo was in no mood to baby-sit, so he, Jan, Po Thang, Trouble, and I went to my boat for the night, leaving Topaz with the teenagers. They all wanted to sleep in Rhonda's king-sized bed, which they'd never seen before, and to watch her king-sized television. If they were homesick or traumatized, they sure didn't show it.

Topaz had been interviewing the girls one by one, gathering as much information as she could from them. Every one of them came from impoverished villages on the mainland, where gangs have taken over many rural areas. Topaz was well-schooled in the fates of the villagers' children under cartel control; young men are initiated into their gangs, and the girls sold into prostitution.

Of course, these children didn't know that. They thought they were being taken to work as waitresses in posh resorts, and so did their families. Not that the villagers could do anything about it, even if they somehow knew otherwise.

Topaz told us, from stories reported by rescued children in the States, that soon after they are taken, the girls are forced to write cheerful letters home. and send small amounts of money, so the parents don't suspect their true fate. With no possibility of returning these girls back to their villages under the current conditions, Topaz was busy on the phone and computer when we left, searching for a solution. At least a temporary one.

I called Jenks as soon as we boarded *Raymond Johnson*, trying to remember what implied prevarications I told him last time we talked. Exhausted by the past three days of driving, hiking, spying, and suspense, I didn't want to screw up. Again. Besides, he'd be in La Paz in a couple of weeks, and I'd be able to tell him the happy ending. I hoped.

Jenks was once again off to some meeting, but he had time to fill me in on his schedule and ask me to send him a list of what he could bring down from California. "And, give Po Thang a hug for me. I can hear him panting."

We ended the call and I wiped dawg drool from my phone.

"Hetta, that had to be the most boring conversation I've ever heard between two people who are supposed to be in love."

"I was afraid I'd drop some kind of hint of what was going on here, so I purposely kept it neutral. He can't do anything about it from Dubai, so why worry him? Besides, by the time he gets here, it will all be over. All's well that ends well."

"Or as well as your crap ever does."

"Oh, come on, Janster. We've got this."

"Yeah, well I gotta hankering for another cocoloco in my life. Let's get that."

Cholo, finally off his phone, joined us on the aft deck. He opened a beer from the mini fridge and sat. He had a frown on his face, but then again, that was normal. After our time in France together, working as partners, I was quite familiar with his stone face. After we met I looked up the Mayan gods, and zeroed in on Ek Chuaj, the god of chocolate.

"So, Ek Chuaj, what's up?" I asked, startling him. He grinned that gorgeous grin that changed him from scary to downright darling. "You have been studying my culture? And of course, you chose chocolate. I like it."

His face returned to stone, and he took a hit of beer. "I am afraid I have bad news."

"Oh, great," Jan said with a groan. "We just have *not* had enough of that lately. Okay, let's have it."

"The plan you have made, to follow *Doña Esperanza* and perhaps discover where the birds are being shipped might be a good one, with one major problem. One I should have thought of."

I gave him a finger twirl to get with it, not needing any more suspense in my life right now.

"My sources tell me both the *Doña Esperanza* and its captain are known to have cartel ties. He has never been arrested for a good reason; there is never any evidence. He weights everything he smuggles, and if he even suspects he is being followed, he throws the contraband overboard. In Mexico, no evidence, no crime."

"Those cages will sink like a rock! I have to let the B team know about this, *muy pronto*."

I sent Roger a message telling him about this turn of events. Within seconds I received a return text, acknowledging the new information on the captain's crappy practices.

"Roger says the truck just arrived, and the first load of birds is being stashed below decks. He estimates this shipment is about a quarter of the total, so we might have three more nights before anything major happens. Drew was in the truck with the old man, Eli. The captain helped unload; still no sighting of any more crew on the boat."

Texting him back, I ask what he thought about the depressing information I gave him about the captain's way of dealing with his cargo. I immediately got an answer: **SB**. That's Roger-text for *Stand By*.

After a few minutes, my text alert chimed. **Not good. Thinking about an alternative plan.**

I told Jan and Cholo what Roger said, then I asked Cholo, "How about you? Do you have any ideas? Looks like we can't take the chance of letting that boat leave Puerto Escondido. But how do we stop it without endangering the birds?"

Cholo gave me the famous Mexican shrug. Not exactly the reaction I wanted.

Jan unfolded her annoyingly lanky body from the settee, strode to my dinette/office in the galley and returned with a large chart book. Flipping it open to Puerto Escondido, she spread it out on the table.

I tapped my finger on the dock's location. "This is where *Doña Esperanza* is side-tied to the muelle."

Cholo picked up the chart, went to his cabin, and shut the door without saying a word.

"You're welcome!" Jan shouted at the door.

What can I say? Good help can come in surly packages.

Cholo rejoined us several cocolocos later, and asked, "What is your fuel level?"

"Mine? Or the boat?"

He eyed the empty pitcher and shook his head. "The boat."

"Topped off."

"Can you reach Puerto Escondido without refueling?"

"Yes, and it's a good thing. There's no other place between here and PE to get diesel."

"We leave at dawn," he said, and left the boat.

Jan hoisted her drink. "Looks like we leave at dawn. Should we run to the grocery store?"

"Yep, I have a feeling we'll have to feed the entire team soon. Especially if we have to leave PE in a hurry for some reason."

"In that case, we'll need several cases of wine."

"I'll drink to that."

Chapter Twenty-seven

AFTER ORDERING US to prepare *Raymond Johnson* to make way for Puerto Escondido at dawn, Cholo left for parts unknown, and we hired Rafael Taxi to take us to Walmart, since they have one of the best wine selections in La Paz. And if Rafael drove, we could take our drinks with us.

"I hope to hell Cholo comes back with a boatload of large guns, or guys," Jan whispered while Rafael chauffeured us in his van.

"Or both. Well, at least Roger and Craig have the gun stash Topaz lifted from Rancho Los Pajaros. Meanwhile, we have to get my tub ready to sail. When we get back, it's stash time, bilge to bridge. Gotta secure anything that will move. If it can, it will. You know the drill."

She gave me a mock salute. "Aye aye, *mon capitan*."

Back on the boat, with enough boxes, bags, and crates to provision the Queen Mary—note to self: do not drink and shop—I handed Jan a copy of my GETTING

UNDERWAY checklist.

"I'll take *numero uno*, CHECK THE WEATHER. Not that it matters, because we have to leave, no matter what. This time of year, we could get lucky and catch a southerly."

"Yeah, right," she said. "When pigs fly."

"Say, Jan," I said as we motored by the islands north of La Paz early the next morning. "Are those sea gulls out there, or pigs on the wing?"

She took a sip of her third cup of coffee and grinned. "Smart aleck. Did we get lucky or what? This weather is perfecto. Oh, look, we have company."

Po Thang, who'd been snoozing at my feet, jumped up and put his paws on the helm. Spotting the source of splashing, he took off for the bow and began barking friendly barks at a small pod of dolphins. They responded by turning on their sides, looking at him, and then leaping into the air.

"I'm always afraid he'll fall in," Jan said, taking in what looked like Po Thang's precarious stance on the bowsprit, which projects over the water a good three feet.

"Never has. He'll settle down in a minute."

As if on cue, Po Thang stretched out on the deck, head on the toe rail, and watched the show, only barking when one of the frisky dolphins splashed him.

"What is the matter?" Cholo yelled as he rushed to the flying bridge to join us.

"Sorry we woke you up. It's nothing but dolphins. Have some coffee. I put the carafe, cream, and sugar in the aft deck sink, just in case we hit a wake. I doubt it though, we haven't seen another boat since we left La Paz."

He took a look around and sighed. "It is so beautiful."

And he was right. The Sea of Cortez is always an amazing sight, but on a day like we were having, the combination of the clear turquoise water juxtaposed against red cliffs, and perfect white sand beaches? The stuff travel brochures are made of.

The hoped-for southerly was light and predicted to last for at least another day. Plenty of time to get to Puerto Escondido and...do what? We still weren't certain, but at least we would all be there on scene, ready and willing to act.

After some time, the dolphins lost interest in us and peeled off, much to Po Thang's disappointment. Jan went below to make sandwiches, and Cholo joined me on the bridge.

"This is a fine vessel. You are lucky to be able to enjoy our beautiful country from the sea."

"I know I am. I just wish Jenks could be here all the time with me."

"Soon enough, I am sure. I miss Rhonda, as well."

I had only seen Cholo once or twice since we all returned from France, but it was obvious he and our friend Rhonda had a thing going. Exactly what *kind* of thing, I wasn't positive, but this was the first time he spoke of her this way.

"When is she coming back to Mexico?"

"Soon. Her mother's house is now sold, so she is only storing some items, and packing a few to bring. Our speed is good for a dawn arrival," he said, pointing at the GPS display while abruptly changing the subject.

I spent the next few minutes familiarizing him with the bridge's instruments, and we worked out our watches. I made the decision, since I couldn't stay on watch all day and night, to take us outside my normal route, and instead of threading between the Baja mainland and a smattering of islands, we'd be at sea, clear of everything. We'd cut back in toward land at dawn the next day, and on into Puerto Escondido.

An overnighter anywhere in the Sea of Cortez under an almost full moon and flat seas is a magical experience, so I didn't plan to miss most of it by sleeping. I chose to take one-or two-hour naps. Jan is familiar with the boat, but not comfortable taking the helm alone at night, and while Cholo was probably more qualified than I to operate a large vessel, he didn't exactly jump at the chance to take over.

Trouble, who had taken a few voyages aboard, was seemingly content to stay in his cage in the main cabin. Probably had something to do with a past dustup with a sea gull or two while underway.

Cell service was ever more sketchy the more northward we traveled, so after we left La Paz we switched to my bajillion pesos a minute SatFone. Cholo was very impressed that I had such a high-tech gizmo and pleased that we could keep in touch with everyone involved while underway. I didn't tell him I'd gouged

Nacho for the system when he hired me for a project he was ramrodding involving giant squid.

We had no idea who Cholo was in constant communication with, but little did he suspect we have a tracer on my system that has saved our bacon on occasion when tracking down suspicious characters, or anyone who makes a call, sends an email, texts, or even farts while using my SatFone.

Just kidding about the farting; it's almost always Po Thang anyhow.

That's my story and I'm stickin' to it.

We all stayed up most of the night, despite our plan to change watches. It was just too fantastical outside to sleep. We had to bundle up against the cold, but with a waning moon still bright enough to allow reading a book on the flying bridge, flat seas, and an abundance of critters to entertain us, we figured what the hell, we'd catch up on sleep once we arrived at Puerto Escondido. The slight southerly and incoming tide gave us a push, and we actually arrived at the outer islands early, so we slowed down and enjoyed breakfast before arriving in PE at dawn.

Roger and Craig, who were keeping watch on the *Doña Esperanza*, told us Eli had managed to leave a note for them at a pre-designated spot, alerting to the fact that tonight's load would be the last. And that Drew planned to accompany the shipment.

There went any hope of those naps.

At first light we hovered outside Isla Danzante,

watching the morning show. The clear water teamed with diving pelicans, jumping dolphins, and a manta ray or two looking like Batman soaring from the water's surface, flapping their enormous wings to knock off parasites, then plunging back with splashes large enough to rock our boat.

To the east, the blood red rising sun painted the western Gigante mountains pink and red, including King Kong peak, named for its resemblance to the big gorilla's profile.

Cholo, who said he'd never seen Puerto Escondido from the water at dawn, was snapping photos and singing its praises. "It is magnifico," Cholo said. "We Mexicans sometimes forget, or take for granted, the beauty of the Baja peninsula."

"It never ceases to amaze me," I agreed. "When I was anchored over there," I pointed to the northeast end of the anchorage through a low berm, "I didn't have to get up early, but I did, just to see this."

Jan, who was also snapping photos, said, "I hate to be the party pooper here, but we'd better get underway."

"Agreed. The waiting room is usually pretty much packed this time of year, but I've made contact with friends who have a large ferro cement sailboat anchored very near *Doña Esperanza*. They say we're welcome to side tie to them temporarily, so unless the weather goes to hell we're set until tomorrow morning. That way, we'll have the port side of the smuggling boat under surveillance, while Craig and Roger have his starboard in their sights from land.

"Yep," Jan said, "we'll have the bastard surrounded."

"Are we ready to smite the enemy?" I said.

"You bet your sweet bippy."

Cholo nodded, then asked, "What is a sweet bippy?"

Jan and I laughed and she told him, "We have no freakin' idea. It was from an old TV show. I think it's a polite way to say *your sweet ass.*"

"Ah. Then yes, I am prepared to bet my sweet ass."

We all fist bumped then Cholo said, "But I must remind you, this captain we are dealing with is a very bad man. He has no heart. He will dispense of the evidence if necessary. I would also bet he has already weighted the cages with rocks or cement blocks, just in case he has to throw them in the sea."

"How do you know so much about him?"

"I was on a recovery team when we found dozens of cages of exotic birds under many feet of water. It was thought they came from this same vessel. We could not prove it, but I, for one, want to catch him this time before it is too late."

Trouble acted like he had understood Cholo. Shaking his head, he shrieked, "Too late! Ack! Too late!"

Jan had a tear in her eye. "Not if we can help it, Pretty Bird."

"Trouble is a pretty, pretty, pretty, pretty—"

I took his cage into my cabin and threw a blanket over it. Those *prettys* can go on for a long time, and the last thing we needed was to catch the attention of that piece of ca-ca, Captain Heartless, upon entering port.

Chapter Twenty-eight

DEPENDING ON YOUR location, phone service can be touch-and-go at Puerto Escondido, and until we felt it was safe to go ashore for a meet-up with Craig and Roger, we sparingly used our walkie talkies, and VHF radios on channel 88, for communication. Even then, in case the *Doña Esperanza* had her radio set on SCAN, we used a kind of unpracticed code to keep in touch.

Before entering port, I called on Channel 88. "H to base, how copy?"

"Loud and Clear."

"Did our provisions arrive last night?"

"That's affirmative. A little ahead of schedule. One or two more shipments expected."

"I read you. Might come to shore later. Say, around nine?"

"We'll keep an eye out. Out."

Cholo and Jan had monitored the conversation, and she let out a war cry that sent Po Thang and Trouble dashing for cover. "We get to take out the bad guys tonight!"

"Calm down, Amazonia. One step at a time. Let's size up the situation before you start lopping off…whatever."

"Spoilsport. Okay, one of us needs to go ashore when we get in. But how? Certainly not in the banana boat."

I was now regretting painting my new *pangita* I use for a dinghy bright yellow. And if that didn't stand out enough, *Johnson Jr.* was stenciled in large letters the length of the nine-and-a-half-foot skiff. Jan and I had a grand old time coming up with that name. Johnson. Banana. Use your imagination.

Yes, my dink was unlikely to be stolen, but now it stood out way too much to use in the anchorage without being noticed.

We glided alongside *Endless Sunshine*, my friends' large cement sailboat, and tied off without fanfare. They were anchored fore and aft, so once we were secured, we were partially hidden from *Doña Esperanza*. I say partially, because my flying bridge loomed above the sailboat, but not enough to cause much notice in the crowded anchorage.

Our main danger was getting clobbered by one of the high-octane sport fishing yachts racing out of port, with little regard for others. They have a bad habit of overlooking the international rules of slowly cruising through an anchorage. I hoped the jerks had learned a lesson in courtesy after one of them plowed into the built-like-a-tank cement boat one day just before dawn. Cement trumps Fiberglas almost every time.

We only had one kayak on board. I am probably the worst kayaker in the world, and Cholo was unknown to our friends on shore, so Jan won a trip to shore by default. Po Thang insisted on going along, Puerto Escondido being one of his favorite haunts.

Dressed in a long-sleeved shirt, baggy pants, a huge hat and giant sunglasses, Jan sort of didn't stand out—which rarely happens—so what would have been an unremarkable scene of someone kayaking was blown all to hell with a large furry critter taking up the back seat.

We spies can't have everything.

While Jan was gone, I fired up the SatFone again, even though we were picking up the internet complements of *Endless Sunshine*, I called Topaz, back in La Paz.

"We're here, and it looks like tonight's show time."

"You're fading in and out, but got that. I'm just now passing through Constitución, so will be there shortly."

"Jeez, you sure got an early start. Please tell me you don't have the Giggle Girl Gang with you."

"Nah, I couldn't stuff 'em all in your pickup. They're in good hands at a nunnery until their future is secure."

"Poor kids. Life has certainly handed them a crappy hand."

"They miss their families but are thrilled to even have their own beds. Their village is dirt poor and has no running water, and certainly no TV. La Paz seems like Disneyland to them. Thank goodness we got them before they were harmed. I did hear Drew tell the goons at Rancho Los Pajaros that if they touched one of them, he'd kill them. I gotta give the bastard brownie points for that. Maybe I'll only remove *one* of his *huevos* with a dull knife. And he did feed Po Thang. Okay, I'll do him a favor and just kill him outright."

"And who says you aren't all heart? But you're gonna have to get in line. Both Jan and Cholo are gunning for him. She just kayaked ashore to meet with Craig and Roger, and to put eyeballs on that piece of crap boat captain. Hopefully she'll come back with a solid plan for tonight. The only sure way we can communicate with Base Camp is by radio."

"You want me to stay with Roger and Craig, or get a ride out to the boat?"

"Don't know yet. Cholo is the only one of us who hasn't been seen by Drew, so maybe we'll send him in and you can come out here. By the time you arrive, we'll know more."

"Okay, *hasta!*"

Jan was gone for an hour-and-a-half while I fretted. I hate being out of the loop, but I had no choice. Cholo kept asking me questions about the anchorage and then calling someone I hoped like hell headed up an entire platoon of really, really bad-assed operatives.

Yeah, right. Smuggling a few birds was small potatoes in the grand scheme of things in a country where nearly 30,000 murders were "reported" last year. Mostly only because it was hard to ignore the bodies. Lord knows how many went *un*-reported! And they have a staggering rate of 98% unsolved. Or even anyone arrested. Birds? Schmirds.

"Oh, Boy! Oberto! Ack!"

Speaking of birds, Trouble's demand for jerky called me inside. I closed all openings in the interior before setting the beast free. He fussed at me some, then settled down with a claw full of jerky. Once he'd polished it off, he surveyed the cabin and barked.

"Sorry, Trouble, he's not here, he went for a walk. You want a nice shower?"

He flew to the sink and waited on the edge while I ran the water, which was already warm from being underway. Once I was certain it was just right, I turned off the hand shower and he jumped in. Trouble immediately went in his fluffing, preening, and singing mode. Yes, my parrot sings in the shower.

Cholo left his cabin to see what all the noise was about and laughed when he saw Trouble, wet and bedraggled, strutting and singing the "Eyes of Texas."

"What else can he sing?"

"Not sure I've heard his entire repertoire. He continually comes up with new ones."

Cholo broke into song with a surprisingly beautiful voice. I was always amazed at how Mexican men sang at will, whether working, drinking, or just because they felt like it. I knew the chorus of "Cielito Lindo" by heart, and joined in.

Ay, ay, ay, ay,
Canta y no llores,
Porque cantando se alegran,

Cielito lindo, los corazones.
(Ay, ay, ay, ay,
Sing and don't cry,
Because singing, they brighten up,
Lovely sky, the hearts.)

But then Cholo sang a verse I wasn't familiar with:
Pájaro que abandona,
Cielito lindo, su primer nido,
Si lo encuentra ocupado,
Cielito lindo, bien merecido

I held up my hand in a break sign. "Nice voice, Cholo. Can you give me a quick translation of that verse? I know *Cielito Lindo* means heavenly sweet one, so evidently the dude has messed up and lost her to another?"

"*Exacto.* It says that a bird who abandons his first nest, the heavenly one, then finds it occupied by another, deserves to lose it."

"You sing it like you feel it. Any story there?"

He sighed. "I was very young and foolish. This song is a reminder to all. If you have your one love for life, do not lose it to foolishness."

I could almost hear Jan saying, "*Got that Hetta?*"

Yes, I got it. After this caper was over, I was going to reform. Not take chances that might send Jenks away. I wouldn't li—prevaricate, to cover my shenanigans. I would—

Again, Jan spoke in my brain, "*Oh, look. Another*

porker just flew by."
I had to get some new friends.

Chapter Twenty-nine

AS A GREETING to Jan and Po Thang when they returned, Trouble shrilled, "Ack! Ack! Ay, Ay, ay, ay, ay! Ay, ay, ay, ay! Ay, ay, ay, ay! Ay, ay, ay, ay—Ack!"

Po Thang howled then lay down with his paws over his ears. Cholo fled to his quarters and slammed the door. I put in my ear plugs. Auntie Jan headed for the jerky stash, which caught both Trouble and Po Thang's attention, and threw a handful at them. Blessed silence ensued.

Cholo emerged just as our VHF radio crackled to life. "Base to Dog House. Switch."

Jan picked up our handheld two-way and answered. "Base?"

"We got some kind of action, right here in river city."

All three of us rushed to the bridge—make that four; Po Thang beat us up there, slipping making it past me as I shut the door to corral Trouble—and we didn't need binoculars to see the problem. A Mexican military convoy was rolling into the open area right behind Base Camp.

"Cholo, are those your guys?" I asked.

"No, my men won't arrive until later today. And they certainly would not make themselves so visible. I must make a call."

"SatFone's already on. We'll stay up here and stand watch."

The convoy was led by several camouflage painted, military grade hummers, packed with machine-gun-wielding troops in full combat gear, their faces covered in black balaclavas. "Whoa baby. That looks serious. Jeez look at that big mother," I said as a really mean looking vehicle rolled into view.

Cholo had just rejoined us and said, "My people are making inquiries. I must contact them in fifteen minutes."

I pointed to the big bad machine, and asked him, "What the heck is that? I think I want one."

"It is a French built *Engin à Roues.*"

I laughed. "It sure as hell looks like one." I'd misunderstood what he said, thus the giggle. I later learned that an *Engin à Roues* is a weaponized wheeled vehicle, while what I heard was *roués*, as in male debauchees. Rakes. Bounders. But perhaps I was giving the French too much credit for a sense of humor?

The Mexican flag-festooned convoy took a turn into a vacant lot, but that gun turret on the roué swung around, aiming straight at me. A little paranoid, you might ask?.

The dust storm they raised blew in our direction, causing us to pull our sweats and jackets over our noses. Po Thang sneezed and jumped off the bench seat behind us, hiding below the dust as it coated us. When the air cleared, we saw at least twenty various vehicles had formed a circle, and two men were hoisting a huge Mexican flag in the center, while others packed sandbags around it for stability.

"Gee Jan, there was a time when all that testosterone would a set our little hearts aflutter. Remember Fleet Week in the Bay area?"

"How could I forget? You almost got us thrown in jail."

"Good thing you had a business card on you. Prostitutes? I mean, *really*. We never, ever, got paid."

"More's the pity."

Cholo shook his head. "Gringas!"

"Don't you have a phone call to make?" Jan drawled

He was only gone a few minutes and was about to tell us what he'd learned, when a helicopter gunship with *Marina*—Navy—and a Mexican flag painted on its side, barely cleared the hill behind us, and then hovered low over the water. Way too close.

As a result of the rotor's downwash, canvas, cushions, and all manner of debris flew off boats, as salt water spray stung our skin and saturated the air.

Jan snatched slickers for us from a flying bridge locker. Po Thang fled for the safety of the covered back deck, and Cholo growled, "Chit!" It was his favorite new English word.

"Chit, as in they are being rude, or chit as in what you learned on the phone?" We were having to yell to be heard over the helicopter noise. I wasn't worried the groady captain could hear us. The roar was deafening.

"Both. I am told this is a scheduled Mexican military exercise. Nothing to do with the ship or our birds."

"Well, for cryin' out loud." Jan yelled. Her face was mud-spattered from a coating of red dirt followed by salt spray.

"We oughta send them a bill for cleaning up this boat. We're coated from stem to stern. Oh, well, no harm, no fou—"

The walkie-talkie hissed and I had to plug my other ear to hear. "Dog House! Dog House! Base!"

"Dog house here. Over."

"The captain just—"

I could barely hear him, but I didn't need to. With a cloud of black smoke, and a mighty roar, the big diesels on *Doña Esperanza* fired up.

Jan screamed, "We gotta stop him!"

"We have to stop him!" Roger yelled in my ear almost the same time.

"Chit."

"We're getting underway!" I started *Raymond Johnson's* engines, and hollered, "Let go the lines!"

Cholo and Jan gave me a thumb's up that they heard me over the helicopter's noise, and quickly untied us from *Endless Sunshine,* while Po Thang ran around the decks, barking like crazy.

Thankfully the 'copter veered off, and I told Jan, "Please secure that mad dog!"

She grabbed him as he ran by her, muscled him inside, and let him howl to his heart's content.

Blanket or not, Trouble was squawking his little lungs out. "Ack! May Day! May Day!"

There was no time to waste. If that rat bastard captain escaped the harbor, he was going to start tossing birdcages overboard, for sure. By the time the navy caught him, as they had in the past, there would be no evidence. Like Cholo said, in Mexico, no evidence, no crime. That's why this jerk wasn't in jail, along with 97% of his fellow miscreants.

"Hetta, what are you going to do?" Jan yelled from the lower deck as she pushed us away from *Endless Sunshine*.

My friend, George, who was helping Jan and Cholo push my boat away from his, yelled, "What's up?"

I knew he was an experienced diver so I waved my mic in the air. "Go 88. Cancel that, Go 72!" I said, knowing most of the boats in the anchorage monitored that channel, and any need for secrecy just bit the dust.

"Got it!"

George went to his cockpit radio. "*Raymond Johnson*, are you declaring a Mayday?"

"No. Yes. That's my parrot doing it, but he's right. We have a mayday situation."

I was stretching it a bit. A Mayday! call indicates a life-threatening situation, as opposed to Pan! Pan!; an urgent situation not immediately life-threatening, but requiring assistance. Semantics.

I took a deep breath and broadcast for all to hear, "Mayday! Mayday! Mayday! The fishing boat tied to the *muelle*, the *Doña Esperanza*, is preparing to leave the harbor with a load of illegal exotic birds. It is our belief that if the captain escapes the harbor, he will throw the caged birds overboard. They will sink and drown. I need every diver in the anchorage to get out here. I'm going to block his exit with *Raymond Johnson*!"

Endless Sunshine replied, "Not alone, you aren't!"

Chapter Thirty

I QUICKLY MANEUVERED *Raymond Johnson* clear of *Endless Sunshine* and aimed for *Doña Esperanza*. Bowing in right in front of him, I held us there with my engines.

Endless Sunshine left his bow anchor in place, loosed the stern hook, and while his girlfriend let out scope, he backed toward the fishing boat's midships, then swung on the fast current directly across the harbor entrance.

He missed me by inches, but we'd set up a pretty effective temporary blockade. There was still room for the captain on *Doña Esperanza* to pull an end-run but he was going to have to back out, then weave through a few boats first because, between *Endless Sunshine* and *Raymond Johnson,* we blocked his main escape route.

I was concentrating on holding the boat in place when Jan yelled, "Hetta, Topaz is here!"

Sneaking a quick glance, I watched as Topaz skidded to a stop no less than twenty feet from the *Doña Esperanza* and jumped out, an AK-47 in hand. Roger and Craig, armed and pissed off, were with her.

I felt a pang of assault weapon envy.

Captain Bastard, realizing he was in deep ca-ca, disappeared below and returned lugging a cage stuffed with crimson and hyacinth macaws, which he dangled over the side. In the bottom of the cage were two cement blocks.

We were close enough for one of us to jump onto the fishing boat, but we waited, afraid he'd drop the birds over the side. Likewise, if we shot him.

The huge beautiful birds were so frantic they were biting each other. The cacophony was ear-splitting, but hope sprang into my heart when the man, obviously fatigued from holding all that weight, pulled the cage onto his boat.

Cholo quickly took aim, but the man had rested the heavy cage on a gunwale and it almost tipped overboard. He caught it at the last minute and yelled over his shoulder and through the open door of the starboard side bridge. He'd spotted Topaz, who actually had one foot on his port deck, and demanded she back off. She did.

For a few minutes we all froze in place, uncertain who should do what next.

"Hetta, we got divers!" Jan pointed to a flotilla of dinghys headed our way, many of the boaters already in wet suits. My depth sounder read fifteen feet, so retrieving a heavy cage before the birds drowned was going to be quite a feat, but I was convinced it could be done.

Cholo went below and came back in nothing but his tighty whiteys, holding an armful of inflatable fenders that we'd used as buffers between *Raymond Johnson* and *Endless*

Summer. He told Jan to take his gun and jumped into the drink.

Jan handed me the Springfield XDM, ran back to the main deck, and began tossing every fender we had overboard, including two large round mooring balls.

Within minutes, while the captain and Topaz traded threats, Jan had opened our dive locker, suited up, and prepared to join Cholo and about ten divers who were gathered on the port side of my boat, hidden from *Doña Esperanza*'s captain.

We had ourselves another maddening impasse. The captain couldn't drop the cage without losing his bargaining chip, and we couldn't nail him without him dropping the cage.

I knew for certain that I couldn't miss a target at such close range with Cholo's XDM, but it was too chancy.

And if I wasn't frustrated enough, Jan yelled, "Uh, Houston to Hetta, we have a problem."

"Lawdy, what now?" I was physically tiring from jockeying the boat, holding it against the swift side current, and mentally pooped.

"Take a look." She pointed toward the military encampment, where every eye in the entire convoy was focused on our brouhaha at the dock.

"Cholo, you better come up here," I hollered over the side. He climbed the swim ladder, where Po Thang greeted him, wagging his tail and licking salt water from his legs. Once on the flying bridge, he took one look at the military encampment and growled, "Chit!"

Trying my best to avert my eyes from his wet whiteys, I said, "Chit indeed. All those soldiers, sailors, and marines can see is a Mexican-flagged ship being bullied by a bunch of Gringo boaters. You gotta go talk to them, pronto! And Jan, get all the divers on board and have them sit on the side away from *Doña Esperanza*. Looks like the chit is about to hit the prop."

Cholo took a minute to pull on home jeans and jumped into my dinghy for a quick ride into shore. He took a handheld VHF radio with him so we could keep him up to snuff, and warn him if he was in danger as he made the five-minute run to the far end of the *muelle*, behind *Doña Esperanza*. He landed, tied off, and sprinted for the military encampment.

I held my breath, hoping the soldiers didn't shoot what looked like a half-dressed, wild man coming their way.

The boat captain was watching Cholo, who was yelling and waving his arms as he ran. I could almost see a light bulb go on over the *pendejo's* head. He looked from me to my dinghy, gave me an evil grin, took a loop on the rail with the line precariously holding the bird's cage, stepped backwards inside his bridge, and threw *Doña Esperanza* into full reverse.

The powerful diesel engine made a high-pitched whine as he reversed toward my shiny yellow pangita, I was temporarily nonplussed, and at a loss for my next move. Just before he hit *Johnson Jr.* he expertly stopped his momentum with his engines, grabbed the cage, ran to the aft of his boat and stepped off into my precious baby panga.

Which Cholo had left idling.

If he escaped the anchorage in Johnson Jr., he could be miles away in no time—with my fifteen horsepower Evinrude flat out, the mini-panga can get on up a plane and do twenty miles an hour or more.

Recovering from my momentary shock at this sudden turn of events, I yelled, "Everyone hang on!" and jammed my own boat into reverse, threw the wheel full over, and hit the throttles.

Jan, realizing what I was about to do, ordered, "Divers! Prepare for emergency underwater rescue! Jump. Now!"

Was I really about to ram my yacht into my own dinghy? What would the insurance company say? Wasn't there a better way out?

From my high perch, I had the best view in the anchorage. Captain Despicable had to place the birdcage into the dinghy and move back to the outboard in his haste to escape. In a split-second decision, I said a little prayer that all the divers were out of my way, put my boat into forward gear, cringing at the ungodly racket of protesting machinery as I used my engines as a brake without going into neutral first. Boats do not like this.

Hitting the emergency ALL STOP button Jenks had installed on the bridge to kill the engines, I turned around, braced myself on the back of my captain's chair, drew a bead on the fleeing captain, and squeezed the trigger four times in quick succession.

The semi-automatic ejected hot brass onto my fiberglass deck and bare feet.

Note to self: repaint bridge deck.

Second note to self: Do *not* shoot while barefoot.

Chapter Thirty-one

"HETTA! HETTA! Are you all right?" Jan screamed from below. "Cease fire!"

She rushed the flying bridge to find me frozen in place, the XDM still in my hand.

"What the hell? Hit the deck."

She pushed me flat behind the steering station while more shots rang out. "Did I get him?" I asked, when the gunfire suddenly stopped.

"I dunno. Do you think you did?"

"Is there a cow in Texas?" I pocketed my spent cartridges and stood to take a look. My target was slumped over while my pangita, with the Evinrude outboard still in gear, made slow circles in the anchorage. "Jan, the birdcage! It's gone!"

Just as I said that, three divers surfaced with a cage full of sopping wet birds. Only the putt-putt on my outboard engine broke the eerie silence in the anchorage until first one, then another bird shook and began squawking their displeasure by raising all Billy Hell. A cheer echoed throughout the anchorage, and on land.

"Bring the cage over here," I yelled. "Fast. We have to get them warm and dry."

Jan keyed the VHF radio. "*Raymond Johnson* to the fleet. Thank y'all! Now can someone please round up Hetta's yellow panga, *Johnson Junior*? It's running in slow circles in the Waiting Room, and the driver seems to have lost consciousness."

She replaced the mic and guffawed. "Lost consciousness? How was that for a tall reach? Yeppers, being shot full of bullet holes will do that to a person every damned time, but I didn't think it prudent to mention that. We saw nothing!"

"I sure didn't, but gotta get rid of this gun, and my .380, before the Mexicans board us. Jump in the kayak and take both of them to Cholo, okay?"

The harbor was suddenly abuzz with boaters coming to the rescue, and the radio waves were so busy they were stepping all over each other. I turned to start the engines again when I felt a bump. We'd drifted between *Endless Summer* and the concrete dock. Seconds later, *Doña Esperanza* gently nuzzled into the log jam of our boats.

Helpful cruisers swarmed around the area in their dinghies like worker bees, fending boats off from each other, re-securing *Doña Esperanza* to the quay, and *Raymond Johnson* right behind her. Under normal circumstances, being tied up to a rough concrete dock wouldn't be my first choice, but this was an emergency, even if my paint job was going to take it in the shorts.

Craig was the first one to leap aboard the minute we were close enough to do so. The wet birds, still in their cage, had been hefted onto my back deck just seconds before, and time was precious.

Some of the macaws were logy, but at least breathing and even screeching in fear and anger. However, others were not so fortunate.

"Hetta, I need a pair of the heaviest gloves you have," Craig said. He was trying to extract the unconscious birds from the cage, but the others were attacking him, and an angry macaw can easily bite off a finger.

Jan ran to a nearby locker and pulled a pair of welder's gloves I'd midnight-requisitioned—construction talk for stolen—from a project site I'd worked on. I keep them on board for emergencies, and this certainly qualified.

Hands and arms protected by thick leather, Craig carefully opened the cage, pulled out unmoving birds, and handed them off to us. "I'll deal with the ones that are raising hell. You guys hold these poor babies by the legs, upside down, and swing them gently between your legs. We're trying to clear their lungs of water, so they can hopefully breathe."

Boaters hovered around, volunteering to help any way they could, but we only had one pair of those heavy gloves, so reaching into a cage full of frenzied birds with huge beaks was a one-at-a-time task. With more volunteers, and more gloves fetched from other boats, the rescue operation picked up speed.

Soon my decks, and the concrete quay, teemed with people swinging eight inverted birds while quietly talking to them in a prayer-like manner, willing them to live. Others stood around until asked to spell those who were tiring from holding the heavy birds. After what seemed an eternity, one large hyacinth coughed, squawked, and bit his Good Samaritan in the butt on the back swing. No good deed goes unpunished.

It took another two minutes until my bird heaved a noise and opened its eyes. "Craig! Mine's breathing!"

"Keep him upside down as best you can until I can deal with him. We gotta get all these big boys inside, out of this breeze. Can someone take the cage into the main cabin? As your birds recover, bring them in and I'll examine them. Hetta, I'll need a ton of towels."

"I'll take the cage, and get towels," Roger told him.

I bit my tongue before telling Roger to leave the expensive towels in my head alone. Oh well, add new towels to that new carpet, and paint job.

Small price to pay for nailing that *pendejo* smuggler, Captain Despicable, and saving the birds.

The encampment's military commander, who had held his troops back instead of turning us into fish food with a free-for-all shootout, was led aboard by Cholo as soon as the wet birds were all recovering inside my boat. They were enjoying warm baths, while their bathers were getting pretty chewed up. My band aid supply was quickly depleted, so the commander called in a couple of medics, and more supplies.

By now we'd drawn quite a crowd, but the six armed and ominous marines posted on the quay kept any non-workers at a distance.

I hadn't had time to even worry about my *Johnson Jr*, or the body in it, but I was told someone snagged it and delivered it to shore. Someone called the Port Captain and he was sure to alert the cops. Thank goodness Jan had palmed off our guns to Cholo during the confusion after the shooting stopped. Until any more officials arrived, it seemed the man in charge was the Comandante, but he was head-to-head with Cholo, talking quietly, so who knew who was really calling the shots?

The rest of us, however, knew the best thing to do was disappear. Unfortunately, that wasn't possible at the moment, so we decided to play stupid. It wasn't hard, as we were stupid-tired.

Jan and I drag-assed after Cholo and the Comandante to the after deck of *Raymond Johnson*, where we all collapsed into cushioned chairs. Not having any idea what Cholo's story had been, we played along—with facial cues from Cholo—the best we could.

Topaz signaled to me from the deck of *Doña Esperanza*, that all birds she found below decks were A-OK. She showed no inclination to join us and faded into the crowd, right past the six marines. Being a woman in Mexico has its advantages at times; if any male had tried that move, they would have stopped him in his tracks.

I offered beer to our little group.

No one declined, dagnab it. I only brought three cases.

We let the Comandante do the talking, since he was officially, albeit somewhat reluctantly, large and in charge. Jan and I drank beer and did our best to appear hapless.

The commandant, who was trained in the United States for some time, asked in accented, but correct English, "Miss Café, when you prevented the *Doña Esperanza* from leaving the harbor, you were trying to rescue your parrot?"

Any lawyer worth her salt would leap to her feet and holler, "Leading the witness!" But we didn't have a lawyer, good or not, and we were quite willing to be led if this was the direction he was going.

Cholo gave me a barely perceptible nod.

"Yes, sir." Uncharacteristically, I did not elaborate, because when I do, I invariably end up hoisting myself by my own petard.

"Hetta," Cholo said as the commandant scribbled something in the notebook he carried, "perhaps you would like to introduce *El Comandante* to Trouble, now that you have retrieved him from those thieves."

"Hoookay," I drawled. *Kidnapped? Well, we* think *he was. At* some *time. By* some*body*.

For a gal who lies at the drop of a hat when the truth will do, I found myself at loggerheads with my second nature.

Cholo's eyes cut toward my main cabin and I jumped up so fast my head swirled. "Yes. Yes, that is an excellent idea." I fled the interrogation.

Retrieving poor Trouble from my master cabin where I stuck him for safety, I put his harness and tether on, and took him outside on my arm.

"Ack! Bad Hetta! Bad!"

"I'm sorry, Honey Bird," I cooed. "Look here, a new friend wants to meet you. Say hello to the nice comandante."

"Ack! *Pinche Puto*!

That insult, along with knowing how much Trouble detests Mexican men, sent Jan's eyebrows reaching for her bangs. "He just talks like that, Comandante," she cooed, flashing some lash. "He doesn't mean you. But, he can be a bit on the unpredictable side, so I wouldn't try to pet him if I were you."

Just in case the man was foolish enough to ignore the warning, I gave Trouble a large piece of jerky to keep his beak of death busy.

Po Thang, who must have heard Trouble, bounded onto *Raymond Johnson* after running right between the legs of a marine. Luckily, the young man—I guess, he had on so much gear it was hard to tell if he was young, or even a he—just laughed.

Po Thang made a bee line for Trouble, who broke the jerky into two pieces, dropping one for his buddy.

"And this is Hetta's dog, Po Thang" Cholo said.

I had not made the introduction, as I wasn't sure I should admit I was his human.

"And a very handsome dog he is," the comandante said, giving Po Thang an ear rub. "Now, is it also true that this dog of yours discovered your bird being held captive upon the *Doña Esperanza?*"

Cholo rotated his finger, and I interpreted it as a go

ahead to embellish.,

"Yes, sir. We were searching for Trouble when my dog pointed to the boat. He is a trained hunting dog."

He made notes again. "And where were you when shots rang out."

Taking aim at the low life in my dinghy?

"I was on my boat."

"Where on your boat?"

I looked at Cholo but he was no help at all.

"I was on the flying bridge," I said, pointing upward.

Cholo nodded approval.

"So you had a good vantage point. Did you see who the shooter, or shooters, were? Or where?"

"No sir. When I heard the first shot, I ducked behind the steering station and hid there."

"So, you have no idea who shot the captain of the *Doña Esperanza*?"

"No, sir!" I clasped my hands to my heart. "Oh, my goodness. Someone shot him?" The practiced prevaricator in me simply couldn't resist the little drama queen move.

Cholo shook his head and closed his eyes. Probably to shut out the view of my smoking britches.

"Yes," the comandante said, "he is…wounded."

"Wounded?" *What? I was sure I plugged him in permanent places.*

Cholo spoke. "The comandante is being…delicate, Hetta. The man has died."

Jan and I chorused "May his soul rest in peace."

And burn in Hell, his roasting flesh being picked from his bones by fire ants, who are certainly from there.

The commandant stood. "I think we are about done here. Perhaps you would not mind to show me your boat papers and identification, just for the record. And allow us to search your boat? It is routine, and my men can use the practice."

Cholo nodded.

"*¡Pásale! Por favor,*" I said with the confident arm-sweep of someone who has ditched her guns. "*Mi yate es su yate.*"

Chapter Thirty-two

THE COMMANDANT'S MEN made a perfunctory search of my boat's interior, which stank of wet parrot, bird vomit, and seawater-soaked carpet, then quickly disembarked. He left two marines to stand guard on the dock, mainly to protect the birds, now that all of them were back on *Doña Esperanza*.

Craig and Roger moved onto the *Doña*, to keep an eye out for the yellow truck that was scheduled to arrive after dark.

Cholo accompanied the comandante back to his encampment, and between the two of them, evidently made short work of dealing with the local cops and the port captain. Within an hour of arriving, they left with a body bag in the back of a pickup. You gotta love Mexican justice: bad guy gets offed by unknown killer and oh, well, he was probably guilty of *something*.

We pushed away from the dock as soon as Topaz came back on board, then we tackled the job of de-stinking my boat. After my brand new wet/dry shop vac overheated for the fifth time, we called it a day; after all, only the main cabin area was affected by the dozen rescued birds, and since my cabin and the guest cabin were still dry and clean, we declared cocktail hour officially official.

We had just settled on the aft deck with cold Tecates (we were too tired to mix anything more exotic) when, miraculously, my phone rang.

I quickly checked the bars: four? *Now* I get four? I vowed to sue Carlos Slim for extreme emotional suffering and trauma due to unreliable phone service.

No caller ID, but this was no time to get picky. The damned thing was working!

"If you're a Nigerian prince asking me to marry you, the answer is yes. Get a pen and I'll give you my social security and bank account numbers."

Jan and Topaz almost spit out their beers.

I can be sooo amusing.

"Café, will you settle for me?" Nacho's unmistakable velvety voice asked.

I mouthed his name, catching the undivided attention of both women. They closed in to eavesdrop.

"Where the hell have you been? We've been through hell up here, and now that it's all *over* you call?"

"You are correct, it is over. Check your email. And please give my best to the lovely Jan and Topaz. "*Hasta luego mi corazon.*"

"I ain't your stinkin' Corazon!" I growled, but he had ended the call.

My friends, who had their ears as close to the phone as possible, heard the whole thing, and we rushed downstairs to get to my computer. I'd made a path over the damp carpet with blue tarps, so we skidded across the living area. I turned on my laptop and we waited impatiently while it booted up.

Since I never knew how Nacho would contact me, I started opening mails I normally would delete as spam.

"Hetta, you know better than to open attachments from unknown sources. Let me read the addresses first, before you get a virus." Jan hip-bumped me out of my chair and cursored down the email list, zeroing in on one from Zorro.

"Gotta be," Topaz said. We all agreed, Jan opened the attachment.

It was a news story out of Mexico City, dated three days before.

Abandoned by the Police, Mexican Villagers Fight to Take Back Their Towns

Just a week after a so-called Comandante X bragged that the cartel's hold on remote villages in Mexico was unbreakable, mysterious paramilitary forces proved otherwise.

His statement in an interview, obviously meant to terrorize anyone who would take on the local cartel, was chilling. "When a cartel commander dies, another one always comes along. The fiesta must continue."

But for at least seven villages in Mexico's southern region, the party is over.

In midnight sweeps, an estimated six hundred cartel henchmen, including the above mentioned Comandante X, were lined up and shot, execution-style, by surprisingly well-armed locals, aided by what they called, "The Zorros."

No one knows what precipitated this attack, but it is rumored that the cartel leaders had taken several young girls from the villages, with an eye to sell them into prostitution, overstepping even the loose morals of the bloodthirsty cartel leaders.

Now that the villages are free of cartel control, the Mexican police and military have moved in, at least temporarily, to ensure they remain so.

However, one frequent tactic used by cartels in the region is to co-opt well-intentioned self-defense groups by gifting them high-grade weapons and cash to win their loyalty.

Only time will tell if these Zorros are the leaders for a bellwether of change for Mexico.

"I take back every single, crappy thing I ever said about Nacho," I said as we high-fived over unbelievably wonderful good news..

Topaz grinned. "Me, too."

Jan, never one to let a chance for gossip go unanswered, gleefully rubbed her hands together. "Topaz, you go first."

Topaz shook her finger at Jan. "Oh, no, you don't. I do not kiss and tell."

"You kissed?"

"Not telling."

Cholo returned before dawn, leaving Craig and Roger to bird sit until they could get the parrots back to the safety of Rancho Los Pajaros.

No matter how much we harassed him, Cholo refused to tell us anything more than that the old truck driver, Eli, was putting as many cages as was safe into his truck and making trips back and forth until the Dona Esperanza was bird free.

We left as soon as we were all on board and arrived in La Paz about the same time as Roger and Craig. They returned my pickup and Jan's Jeep, then hopped a plane back to Arizona.

Cholo vanished, and even Rhonda, when I called her, said she had no idea where he was.

Topaz caught a flight to Mexico City, with plans to visit the girls in their villages. Jan and I suspected she was going to rendezvous with Nacho, as well.

If there is one thing we hate above all else, it's being left in the dark. And on so many levels.

Jan left for the whale camp the day Roger, Craig and Topaz took off.

Po Thang, Trouble, and I were left to deal with a crew of worker bees, who shampooed my wool carpet well enough to save it, touched up the side of my boat where the concrete quay scraped the paint, and the boat was given a stem to stern spit and polish.

Within a few days, it was as though nothing ever happened.

And I planned to keep it that way!
Ha! When porkers take wing.

EPILOGUE

"SO," JENKS SAID, as we lay hand-in- hand on the warm deck of *Raymond Johnson*, drying out after a skinny dip in shallows warmed by the sun-heated sand bottom, "have you heard from that old truck driver, Eli? I mean, since he took all the birds back to the aviary?"

"Yep. He's in charge of the Camp Muleshoe now, and Humberto and Anna are back running Rancho Los Pajaros. Seems after that weird phone call I got from Humberto, that rat Drew actually *did* send the couple to La Paz to stay with family down there."

Jenks had arrived the day before, so we beat feet out of La Paz for the islands. I'd been easing him into the story of the birds, girls, and the like, careful not to divulge anything that would prove me a liar. It wasn't easy.

"Let me get this straight," Jenks said lazily. "Eli, Humberto, and Anna are safe, and the birds are back at the ranch. Looks like Nacho somehow returned the girls to their villages and families after banishing the cartel bad guys?"

"That about sums it up. Except that Mrs. Doctor

Washington is still planning my wedding to Craig."

He chuckled. "You trying to make me jealous?"

"Is that possible?" *Ugh, that sounded like I was fishing for…what?*

"Absolutely. I've had the hots for Craig for ages."

I backhanded his stomach with my wet arm. "Watch it, Buster."

"Okay, I like you much better. Let's get back to this adventure you guys had while I was working away in the deserts of Dubai. Seems to me the only loose thread left, then, is that mule skinner. What happened to him?"

"I have no idea. I know that Roger and Cholo were waiting for him out at the main highway. Jan, Topaz, and I watched for hours, waiting for the old man's yellow truck, but he didn't roll in until midnight, and he was alone."

"Did he say where Drew was?"

"Nah, just shrugged,"

"And a master interrogator like you, couldn't make him spill the *frijoles*?" Jenks joked.

"Nope. Dude is a tough one. Jan was mightily disappointed that dastardly mule skinner wasn't with him. She was dearly looking forward to removing Drew's *huevos*. Very slowly, with something dull."

Jenks squirmed. "Let's talk about something more pleasant, okay?"

"Chicken."

"Ack! Bwak Bwak Bwaaaaaak!"

"Exactly, Trouble."

My bird was perched nearby, out of the sun and

tethered to his cage, but with plenty of leash-length so he could quickly escape inside the wire enclosure, just in case a seagull bully tried picking another fight. The last time he took them on, we were crossing the sea, and his defeat was clearly embedded in his little bird brain.

Po Thang, lounging nearby, opened one eye, and went back to sleep. Being free of the dock, he was back to swimming most of the day, and chasing fish and birds in the small cove where we were anchored all by our lonelies. Heaven.

"You hungry yet?" I asked, reaching over and running my hand through his damp hair.

"Only for you."

I love a man who has his priorities straight.

THE END

Acknowledgements

Holly Whitman has been the editor of every one of my books, and she keeps me out of the ditch when I write myself into one. The last eyes on the book before I hit the "publish" button, are Donna Rich's. Thanks Holly and Donna.

AND, I have some amazing beta readers! I can't tell you how much I appreciate these sharp-eyed readers for catching boo-boos I overlooked. And here they are, in no particular order: Lela Cargill Stephen Brown, Sybil Dean, Bonnie Julian, Karen Kearns. Mary Jordan, Frances Moore, Carmen Repsold, Jeff Bockman, Jenni Cornell, William Jones, Wayne Burnop, Lee Johnson, George Burke, Dan O'Nielle, Karen Hayes, and Krystyna Sews.

From the Author

I want to thank every one of you who take the time to read my books. You are the reason I keep writing, and I wish I could meet you all in person.

If you have enjoyed this book, please tell your friends about Hetta or post a short review on Amazon, Goodreads, heck, anywhere. Word of mouth is an author's best friend and is much appreciated.

Also, you can find me on Facebook at https://www.facebook.com/jinxschwartz.

BookBub also alerts my readers when I have book featured with them, or a new release. You can follow my author page to be notified.
https://www.bookbub.com/authors/jinx-schwartz

I have great editors, but boo-boos do manage to creep into my books, no matter how many talented people look at it before publication. If you find an error, it's all on me. And, should you come upon one of these culprits, please let me know and I shall smite it with my mighty keyboard! Thanks! You can e-mail me at jinxschwartz@yahoo.com

Also, I must thank Sweet Tea Baird, our cover dog. She, like Hetta, is a Texas gal, from Amarillo. Yes, Tea is a female, but in our brave new world, we don't want to discriminate by gender, right? Her full name is "Highmark Wingstar I'll Have Sweet Tea." She is the daughter of Tycho, cover dawg for Just Pardon My French. Wouldn't you just love to live in the Baird household in Colorado, where there always seems to be a new puppy?

Sweet Tea enjoys keeping her Dad and Brother in line. Currently she's working on her Therapy Dog skills, which come naturally. She has a hypnotizing smile and warm heart. But like any good Texas girl, she's no pushover. She's a bit of a Tomboy and keeps those boys in line! Atta girl.

For the fab cover art, I have Karen Phillips to thank, once again.

Books by Jinx Schwartz

The Hetta Coffey Series

Just Add Water (Book1)
Just Add Salt (Book 2)
Just Add Trouble (Book 3)
Just Deserts (Book4)
Just the Pits (Book 5)
Just Needs Killin' (Book 6)
Just Different Devils (Book 7)
Just Pardon My French (Book 8)
Just Follow The Money (Book 9)
Just For The Birds (Book 10)

Boxed Sets

Hetta Coffey Boxed Collection (Books 1-4)
Hetta Coffey Boxed Collection (Books 5-8)

Other Books

The Texicans
Troubled Sea
Land of Mountains

CPSIA information can be obtained
at www.ICGtesting.com
Printed in the USA
LVHW011514060720
659898LV00014B/1426